RAMOSE

STING OF THE SCORPION

CAROLE WILKINSON

About the Author

Carole Wilkinson is an award-winning writer of over thirty books and TV scripts. She is interested in the history of everything and finds the hardest thing about writing books is to stop doing the research. She collects teapots and lives in Melbourne, Australia, with her husband, daughter and a spotty dog called Mitzie.

RAMOSE
STING OF THE SCORPION

CAROLE WILKINSON

CATNIP BOOKS

Published by Catnip Publishing Ltd.
Islington Business Centre
3-5 Islington High Street
London N1 9LQ

This edition published 2006
1 3 5 7 9 10 8 6 4 2

First published in Australia in 2001 by black dog books,
71 Gertrude Street, Fitzroy Vic 3065

A CIP catalogue record for this book is available from the British Library

ISBN 10: 1 84647 006 4
ISBN 13: 978 1 84647 006 6

Printed in Poland

For John and Lili

CONTENTS

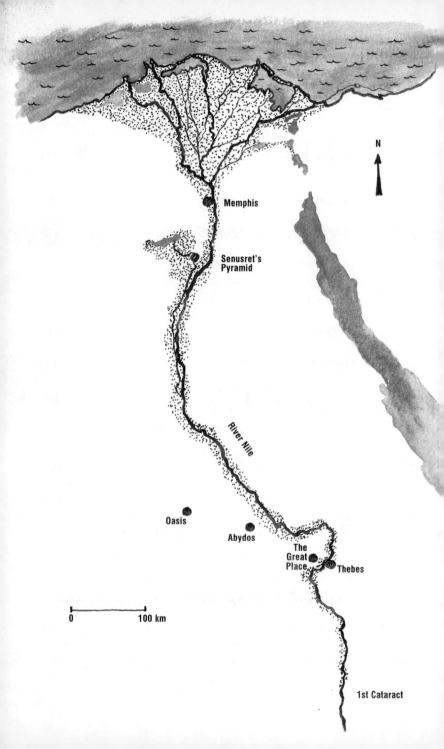

NIGHT IN THE DESERT

"**P**OOR MERY is hungry," said Karoya, stroking her cat. She threw the last pat of donkey dung on the spluttering fire. "She shouldn't be cold as well." The sandy-coloured cat sat as close to the flames as she could without burning her fur.

"We're all hungry," said Hapu grumpily. "But you're more concerned about that cat than us."

"We chose to be here. She didn't," said Karoya.

"Well, if we were travelling along the river we wouldn't be hungry," grumbled Hapu. "We could fish every day."

Ramose's stomach growled. Like the others he had eaten nothing but stale bread and dried figs for the last three days.

"We can't go back to the river, Hapu," said Ramose. "It's too dangerous."

Three days earlier, Ramose had seen men searching the riverbank. He was sure it was the vizier's men looking for them.

"We crossed over the river so that they couldn't find us," complained Hapu. "I don't see why we have to travel in the desert as well."

Ramose had insisted that they leave the fertile Nile Valley and walk parallel to the river but out of sight of the fertile land.

"We attract too much attention," Ramose said. "In Egypt everyone has a job to do, a place to be. Three young people shouldn't be wandering around the country by themselves."

Hapu grunted. He knew Ramose was right.

Ramose stared moodily into the fire. The flames were dying. A handful of reeds and a pat of donkey dung didn't burn for long. He saw a slight movement out of the corner of his eye. As he watched, a pale, creamy coloured scorpion crawled out from under a rock. It was big—more than á palm-width long. It climbed onto the rock and raised its pincers. Its tail curled menacingly above it. Ramose was about to reach out and squash it with his sandal. Then he realised that the creature was warming itself by the fire just as they were. He left it alone.

It was a strange situation for a prince to be in, travelling on foot, hiding in the desert, living like a barbarian. There was a reason why he was doing it though—a good reason. He was going back to the royal palace at Thebes. He had to let his father know that he was still alive. Then he would reclaim his place as Pharaoh's elder son and heir to the throne of Egypt.

It was over a year since one of his father's lesser wives had tried to poison him so that her own son, Tuthmosis, could become pharaoh. Ramose's tutor and nanny had saved him by pretending that he had died. They had hidden him in the tomb makers' village where he lived, as a scribe, for many months.

Karoya was roasting a snake over the tiny fire. That was to be their evening meal.

"I don't see why anybody would choose to live out here," grumbled Hapu. "Why didn't your people live in villages?" he asked Karoya. "Were they running away from someone?"

"No," said Karoya indignantly. "It was the life they chose."

Karoya was the only one who liked travelling close to the desert. It reminded her of her home in Kush, a desert country to the south of Egypt, which had been conquered during Pharaoh's last military campaign.

"But how did you survive?"

"My people knew the desert as well as Egyptians know the river. We kept herds of cattle. We were always moving, seeking grass for the cattle to eat. It was a good life."

Karoya was speaking as if her people didn't exist any more. Ramose knew that she had been captured by his father's army and forced to become a slave. He had never asked her what had happened to her family. He was afraid that the answer would make him ashamed of being Egyptian.

Karoya handed them each a piece of the snake and a gourd of water.

"It's like eating leather," grumbled Hapu, spitting out bits of snakeskin.

The snake was tough and tasteless, but Ramose didn't complain.

He glanced over at the black-skinned slave girl sitting next to him. Without Karoya's knowledge of the desert, Ramose knew they would have died of hunger. Their food supplies had been scanty, but what little they had, Karoya found. She had killed the snake. She had trapped a bird. She organised night-time trips back into the fringes of the cultivated land to collect water, grain and vegetables. Ramose didn't like adding to his crimes by stealing from people's fields and orchards. But they had no choice. He hoped Maat, the goddess of justice, would understand. He promised himself he would make an offering to her as soon as he could.

Hapu didn't know anything about the desert, but he was a loyal friend and good company. He told stories as they walked. Even when Ramose was feeling like he'd never achieve his goal, Hapu could always make him smile. Without his friends, Ramose may well have given up in despair.

"It's your turn to go and get water," Karoya said to Ramose.

Ramose nodded. He no longer thought it strange that a prince should do as a slave girl told him. Back in the palace, servants weren't even allowed to look him in the eye, let alone tell him what to do.

He took the water-skin and walked towards the fertile land. Thoth, the moon god, hadn't risen yet, but Ramose used the stars to guide him. It took him an hour to reach the first fields of the cultivated land. He found an irrigation canal surrounding a field of beans. He filled the water-skin and picked some beans as well.

By the time he got back to the camp, his friends were asleep. They had arranged their reed mats around the little fireplace—even though the fire had gone out. Karoya was wrapped in the length of faded cloth that she wore over her head. She was curled around Mery for extra warmth. Hapu only had a coarse linen shirt. Ramose wrapped himself in the woollen cloak that had been with him ever since he left the palace. It wasn't enough to keep out the cold of the desert night.

Two hours later, Ramose was still awake. The sand was as hard as a block of stone. He turned onto his back and stared up at the night sky. The stars in their millions twinkled above him.

In his head, Ramose ran through the events of the past weeks again and again. If he'd done things differently they wouldn't be in such a miserable state. A month ago, a high priest had accused them of being tomb robbers and tried to arrest them. They could easily have been imprisoned in Memphis. They'd had a narrow escape.

A wave of shame and anger crept over Ramose. The truth was, he was a tomb robber. He had stolen gold and jewels from Pharaoh Senusret's pyramid. It was the worst crime in Egypt and he was guilty of it. It hadn't been Ramose's choice, though. A gang of tomb robbers had kidnapped him and they had forced him to crawl into the heart of the pyramid and steal the gold and jewels from the tomb. Hapu had fallen into their clutches as well. The two boys had been abandoned, trapped underground. Mery had saved them. The cat had led them out of the tomb.

He was sure Vizier Wersu was pursuing them because they were tomb robbers. The vizier didn't know it was Ramose who had robbed the tomb. He, like everyone else, thought that Ramose was dead. That was the way Ramose wanted it to stay.

Ramose removed a sharp stone from under his back. He sighed and turned on his other side. He felt something prick his leg. He shifted again with annoyance. Would he ever get to sleep?

As he lay there, a swarm of mosquitoes suddenly attacked him. He couldn't see them, but he could feel them biting him all over. Then a tall, thin man with a face like a crocodile appeared from nowhere. He had his long, white robes draped over one arm as he walked. Even in the darkness, Ramose knew who it was. It was Vizier Wersu. He was holding a bronze statue of Seth in the form of a strange animal with square ears, a pointed snout and a forked tail. Seth was the god of chaos and confusion who had killed his own brother, Osiris, and gouged out the eye of his nephew, Horus, god of the sky.

Seth was an ugly-looking god, but the statue was a beautiful thing. Ramose thought about the cost of such a large bronze statue. It was probably enough to feed three families for a year. He wondered why anyone would want to worship such an unpleasant god. He admired the delicately carved hippopotamuses around the base. It's strange how you can see so much detail in dreams, thought Ramose. And odd how you can feel as well as see. He scratched furiously at the itchy bites all over his body.

The vizier had an evil look in his eye. He took hold of the feet of Seth with both hands and swung the statue as if it were a weapon. It was a weapon. He swung the heavy bronze statue again, aiming it right at Ramose. Ramose rolled out of the way and the statue dug into the sand, narrowly missing his head. He was surprised at the skinny vizier's strength. The vizier raised the statue above his head. Ramose tried to roll out of the way, but he caught his foot in his bag. Vizier Wersu brought down the statue hard on his right leg. It hurt. Ramose cried out in pain.

Then Ramose saw that in his other hand, the vizier held a large fig, the biggest fig Ramose had ever seen. Wersu was trying to force it into Ramose's mouth. Ramose tried to stop him, but he couldn't move because his leg was hurting and his body was itching from the mosquito bites. Wersu hit his leg again with the bronze statue. The pain was terrible. Ramose opened his mouth to scream and the vizier prised open Ramose's jaws and forced the fig in. The huge fruit wedged in his mouth so that he could neither spit it out nor swallow it.

It was cold, so cold. Ramose shivered and shivered and couldn't stop. He felt sick. This is a dream, he told himself. All I have to do is wake up. His eyes were wide open but he couldn't wake up.

The moon god, Thoth, finally climbed into the sky. Ramose was pleased to see the bright disc of the moon. Thoth was also the ibis-headed god of writing, worshipped by scribes. Thoth was only there for a moment before the black sky turned dark orange. The first rays of the sun were appearing over the horizon. Before long the sky was light and the moon faded until it was like a ghost of itself in the morning sky.

Karoya awoke and sat up. Hapu stirred in his sleep. Ramose realised with a jolt that he wasn't dreaming. He was awake. The pain in his leg from Wersu's blow was unbearable. The itching hadn't gone away. And try as he might, he could not swallow the fig jammed into his mouth. He tried to speak to Karoya, but he could only make a terrible animal noise.

Karoya knelt down at his side. Her forehead was creased with concern. She seemed to be shuddering and quivering from side to side. Then

Ramose realised that it was him that was moving. He was shivering violently and couldn't stop.

"Hapu," said Karoya. "Quick, get the water."

Hapu sat up sleepily. As soon as he saw Ramose he jumped to his feet.

"What's happened to him?"

"I don't know, but he needs water. His tongue is so swollen, it looks like he might choke."

What's wrong with me? Ramose wanted to ask as he gulped the water, but he couldn't. He had never felt so sick. He was sweating as if he were lying out in the midday sun, but the sun's rays hadn't yet reached their camp. He couldn't breathe properly. He sucked in gulps of air. His heart was pounding. Karoya was swimming blurredly in front of him.

Ramose felt her hands as she searched his body for signs of injury or illness. She touched his right leg and he cried out in pain.

"Here," said Karoya. "Look. Something has bitten him."

Karoya pulled the cloak away from him. Ramose raised his heavy head and glimpsed his lower leg, which was swollen to the size of a melon. He might have imagined the vizier hitting him with a statue, but the pain was real.

Karoya suddenly snatched up her grinding stone. Ramose flinched as she held it above her head ready to hurl at him. He tried to cry out again. Not you, Karoya. You haven't turned against me, have you? No sound came out, but saliva dribbled from his mouth as if he were a baby. He felt a rush of air as the stone narrowly missed his leg and dug into the sand next to him. What is happening? he wanted to ask. Ramose felt his eyelids droop. His life was in danger, he didn't know what was real and what wasn't, but all he wanted to do was sleep. Karoya knelt down and picked up something very cautiously between her fingers. Ramose's vision was blurry, but he could make out what it was. It was a dead scorpion.

SAND AND MIRRORS

R AMOSE OPENED his eyes. A man with a thin, grim face and a small, straight mouth was looking down at him.

For a moment, Ramose thought that it was Wersu. Then he realised that the face was burnt dark brown and creased like old leather. It was framed by a piece of dark cloth wrapped around the man's head. His black, piercing eyes were bright like a bird's, nothing like the vizier's. As the man reached across to feel Ramose's brow, the boy felt the coarse cloth of a thick, long-sleeved garment scrape against his arm. The man smelt bad, as if he had not bathed for a very long time.

The pain in Ramose's leg was still there, but he wasn't itchy any more. The man held a gourd to Ramose's mouth. Ramose drank from it. The liquid was thick and tasted something like milk, but it was nothing like the milk from cattle or gazelles. It tasted like someone's feet had been washed in it.

Then the man disappeared from Ramose's view. He heard an unintelligible shout and then felt movement. His body was jolted and jarred, as if he were lying on something that was being dragged along the ground.

A piece of coarse, hairy cloth was stretched above him to provide shade from the sun. He could feel the warmth penetrating the cloth. Ramose turned his head to see where he was. Under the edges of the shade cloth he could see nothing but sand.

There was a strong animal smell, so unpleasant it made him feel sick. All around him were animal noises—some that sounded familiar, others that didn't sound like any animal he'd ever known. There were other unfamiliar sounds, irregular clinkings and clankings. His body rocked and lurched as he was pulled along by something unseen.

Ramose was comfortable, despite all the bumping and the smells. He could feel a strong, cool pressure on his right leg, as if there were something heavy weighing down on it. The pain was still there, but it seemed to be somewhere else, as if someone had taken it out and put it down at a distance.

Ramose didn't know where he was going or who was taking him there, but at that moment he didn't care.

He woke again. He was still bumping along. He smelt the strong smell of fresh animal dung. He heard voices, strange sounds made in the back of the throat. The voices made no sense, though. The unknown animal joined in. Ramose tried to sit up but he couldn't. Then the movement stopped. Everything was still.

The shade cloth was suddenly thrown back and there stood Karoya. She was looking down at him with the same crinkled look of concern as when he'd last seen her. Ramose's tongue had shrunk back to something like normal size. He thought he would try and speak.

"Hello, Karoya." His words were a little slurry, but Karoya's black face was suddenly split by a brilliant white crescent as she smiled down at him.

"How are you feeling?" she asked.

"Better," he said. "I saw a strange man."

"That was Zeyd."

Ramose tried to sit up, but couldn't move his arms or legs. He raised his head and saw the reason why he was unable to move. He was tied to a sort of sled.

"Have we been captured by barbarians?" he asked.

Karoya smiled again as she undid the knots. "No. You are tied onto the sled, so you don't fall off."

He looked up past Karoya's bent head and saw what had been pulling his sled.

"I must be still dreaming," he said, as he stared at the strangest creature he had seen in his entire life.

"No, you're not," said Karoya, as she helped him to sit up.

Ramose stared at the creature. It was the biggest animal he'd ever seen. It towered above him. It had large hoofed feet, skinny legs and matted brown hair. On the end of a long, curved neck was the ugliest face imaginable. A big-lipped mouth full of large, yellow teeth moved from side to side as it chewed on some dried grass. Strangest of all, on the creature's back was a large hump.

"What is that?" asked Ramose, unable to tear his eyes away from the ugly creature.

"It is called a camel," said Karoya knowledgeably, holding a gourd of milk to Ramose's lips.

"Why does the milk taste so strange?" he asked.

"It's camel's milk."

As Ramose sipped the milk, he looked around and took in his new surroundings. He didn't have to ask where they were—he could see. They were deep in the desert. Whichever way he looked he could see nothing but sand.

It was not the desert along the edges of the fertile land that he and his friends had been travelling in. There were no rocky outcrops, no occasional tufts of grass. There was no sound of insects, no birds flying overhead. In every direction all he could see was sand—hard flat sand and its surface rippled like a wind-blown pond.

A group of grubby children was standing staring at Ramose.

Ramose whispered to Karoya. "Are you sure we aren't captives?"

Karoya laughed. "No, we are guests. Honoured guests. These people are nomads. Zeyd is their chief. They travel from oasis to oasis to graze their goats. And you don't have to whisper, Ramose. They have their own language and they don't understand a word of Egyptian."

"How do you know so much about them? Can you speak their language?"

"I don't have to speak to them," said Karoya, laughing again. "This is the way my family lived before the Egyptians came." It had been a long time since Ramose had heard her laugh so much.

The nomads were strange-looking people. There were three dark men, all like the one who had leaned over him, all wearing long-sleeved, hairy coats that came down to their ankles. They had pieces of dark cloth wrapped around their heads.

There were also five women and some children. The women had patterns tattooed in dark blue on their faces. They wore heavy beaded necklaces and bracelets. They had rings, not on their fingers, but pierced through their ears and noses. The children were tending a herd of about twenty goats, giving them dry grass from a sack.

It was the strangest sight Ramose had ever seen, but strangest of all was the camel creature. It carried leather saddlebags and rolls of cloth. Large terracotta jars and metal cooking pots hung on either side of the animal's strange humped back.

Ramose realised it was the animal's strong smell that he had smelt as he was pulled behind it. The strange sounds he'd heard were the jars and pots knocking against each other.

Ramose watched as the people made their camp in the desert. They stuck sticks into the sand and draped heavy cloth over them, holding down the edges with stones. In less than an hour there was a comfortable little village: four cloth houses and a cooking fire.

"Don't they want to know who we are, what we're doing?" asked Ramose.

"No. Desert people welcome all travellers." Karoya's eyes shone. "Anyone who comes to their camp is made welcome and given food."

Ramose thought that the children would have been more interested in their strange guests, but they were all huddled around something, laughing and squealing. One of them stood up with the object of their fascination in his arms. It was Mery.

"They have never seen a cat before," Karoya said. "They had never even heard of such a creature."

One little girl, who was no more than four, reached out slowly to the cat. She touched the fur and Mery miaowed. The little girl jumped back in terror. Ramose found it hard to believe that the children could be frightened of a little cat, yet they played happily at the feet of the monster animal they called camel.

"I have never heard of camels," said Ramose.

"It is from a far distant place where there are

many such creatures," Karoya explained. "Zeyd won the creature in a fight with the chief of an enemy tribe. The camel doesn't need to drink like other animals. Zeyd believes that it stores water in the hump on its back. He wishes that he had more camels."

"I thought you said you didn't speak their language."

"I don't. Zeyd explained with his voice and his hands and pictures in the sand."

Ramose inspected his leg, which was bandaged in coarse cloth and squashed under a heavy stone. He lifted off the stone and unwrapped his leg.

"The weight of the stone stopped the poison from spreading to other parts of your body," Karoya explained.

Large leaves were pressed into the area where he'd been bitten. Ramose gently removed them.

"These look like lotus leaves," he said.

"They are. They stop the pain. The leaves are very precious to desert people because they are hard to get. The lotus plant is very useful. There was some powdered lotus in the milk you drank as well."

Ramose's lower leg was still swollen and there were two puncture marks in his calf.

"The poison in desert scorpions is strong and you were bitten twice. If the nomads had not appeared out of the desert," Karoya said quietly, "I think you would have died."

The nomad women lit a small fire using dried palm fronds and dung just as Karoya did. Hapu helped Ramose to his feet and led him to the fire. There was the smell of roasting goat's meat and baking bread. Ramose's stomach growled. It had been weeks since he'd eaten properly.

As soon as the sun dropped below the horizon, it got cold, colder than Ramose had ever known it to be in Egypt. He shivered, even though he was sitting as close as possible to the flames.

Zeyd, the man he had seen earlier, said something to one of the women. She disappeared inside a tent and returned with warm clothes for the guests. Ramose gratefully pulled on a long, hairy garment similar to the other men's—a dark, heavy coat that reached the ground. From the smell of it, Ramose guessed it was made of woven goat hair. He was getting used to the strong smell of goats already, and it was good to feel warm.

They all sat around the fire and ate a meal of goat's meat, bread and a vegetable that Ramose didn't recognise. After that there were dates and warm milk. The nomads talked among themselves in their strange language. The children stared at Mery who was curled up in Karoya's lap. They giggled as Hapu pulled faces and did little tricks for them.

"I can't believe they don't want to know who we are," Ramose said.

"They think that is our business, not theirs," said Karoya.

"How do they know we're not planning to steal their goats?" asked Hapu.

"It doesn't matter. It would be a shameful thing to turn away a traveller in the desert, even if he's an enemy."

"We're not their enemies though," said Ramose.

"Yes, we are," said Karoya. "At least you two are. Egyptians are the enemies of all desert people. They kill them for no reason or enslave them. You especially are their enemy, Ramose."

"Would it make a difference if they knew who I was?"

"No, even the pharaoh's son would be welcome."

Ramose looked around at the nomads. The men were discussing their goats. The women were clearing away the remains of the meal and mending clothes and tents. The children were getting sleepy. The younger ones were already asleep in their mothers' laps.

"How can I thank Zeyd?" Ramose asked Karoya.

"You don't have to," she replied. "He expects that you would do the same for him."

Like most Egyptians, Ramose had never met any barbarians before. He had never imagined that he would one day be accepting their hospitality, enjoying their food and sleeping in their tents.

Ramose offered to sleep outside, but Zeyd refused. Ramose slept a dreamless sleep, more peaceful than any since he had left the Great Place.

They spent the next two days travelling through the desert, seeing nothing but sand. Each morning the tents were taken down, the camel was loaded up and the nomads walked through the desert, herding the goats in front of them. They left behind them nothing but their footsteps and the tent stones, piled together for other nomads to use.

Ramose sat on the sled at first, but by the second day he was able to walk for part of the day. The children took it in turns to carry Mery's basket. Even the smallest insisted on carrying it for a few paces.

The sand stretched out before them flat in all directions. It was hard and, as they walked, their feet made a hollow, booming sound as if they were walking across the stretched skin of a drum. The sun burned down on them and turned the yellow sand to a glaring white.

"I can see water ahead," said Hapu as they walked. "Look, there's a lake!"

Karoya laughed at him. "It's not a lake. It's the sun playing tricks on your eyes."

Ramose could see the shimmering mirage as well, a pool of reflected sky just ahead of them.

"My people call it the devil's mirror," said Karoya.

Ramose shaded his eyes to look at the mirage. They kept walking towards it, but they never got any closer. It was always just ahead of them.

After two days of seeing nothing but flat sand stretching in every direction, two dark dots appeared in the distance.

"Is that another mirage?" asked Hapu.

Karoya shook her head.

As they drew closer, Ramose could see that it was two piles of rocks. Zeyd smiled and nodded when they reached them. The women replaced rocks that the wind had blown from the piles. Then they swept away sand that had built up against them.

"They are signposts," said Karoya. "It means that we are heading in the right direction. The piles of stones are a gateway leading to the road ahead."

Hapu walked between the two piles and looked around him. There was still nothing but sand.

"It looks like a gateway to nowhere," he said.

The nomads laughed at Hapu, even though they couldn't understand what he said.

3

GATEWAY TO NOWHERE

O N THE THIRD DAY, the landscape changed. The sand gradually started to rise and fall. Then it piled up into dunes. The dunes grew bigger and bigger until they were towering above them on either side. The colour of the sand changed too, from yellow to pink to pale purple.

"I didn't realise that sand could be so many

different shapes and colours," Ramose said to Karoya as they walked.

"I told you the desert was beautiful," said Karoya. "You didn't believe me."

"I still wouldn't call it beautiful, but I'm starting to see it a little differently."

Ramose didn't feel threatened by the desert as he had when he first left the Nile Valley. He still couldn't imagine living in it permanently, but it didn't hold the same fears for him as before.

"Do you have any idea where we're going, though?" asked Hapu, joining them as they walked.

"We're walking south, that's all I know," said Ramose, looking up at the sun.

"Eventually we'll have to stop going south and find the river again," said Hapu.

At midday, the nomads stopped for a short while to drink milk and eat bread. Then they continued their journey. Hapu was getting bored.

"Let's play a game," he said enthusiastically.

"If we stop to play, we'll get left behind," said Ramose.

"I was thinking of a game we could play while we're walking," said Hapu. "I'll think of something that we can all see. I'll tell you what sound it begins with and you have to guess what it is."

"It'll be a short game. All we can see is sand!"

"Try it and see," said Hapu. "It'll be fun."

Ramose and Karoya agreed to play the game. Hapu was very inventive and thought of things like sand grain, camel tail and goat's ear. Even so, it didn't take long until they had used every possible thing that they could see. Ramose, whose body was still healing from the effects of the scorpion poison, was happy just to walk and let his mind wander.

His body was still weak, but inside Ramose felt strong. The fact that he had survived the scorpion bite gave him courage. Vizier Wersu had attacked him and he'd survived. He knew that the vizier had only been a vision, that it was really the scorpion that had nearly killed him, but in his mind he felt as if he'd overcome his enemy. He didn't know where the nomads were going, but he knew he was getting closer to Thebes. Every step was taking him closer to his home and his family.

In the afternoon, a breeze picked up. Grains of sand blew gently across the surface of the dunes.

"I'd forgotten what a breeze was like," said Ramose, turning his face towards the faint rush of cooler air.

The nomads didn't seem pleased about the breeze and made the camel walk faster.

The breeze became a wind. The sand started to shift slightly. The wind blew the sides of the dunes into steeper and steeper slopes until they eventually collapsed and cascaded into new shapes. The wind grew stronger and the blowing sand started to sting their hands and faces. The nomads unwound the cloth from their heads and covered their faces with it. The long nomad coats protected the friends' arms and legs. Ramose and Hapu had nothing to shield their faces from the sharp sand. Karoya wrapped her striped cloth over her face. She also took Mery's basket from the children and held it close to her, muttering reassuring words to the cat.

Within an hour, the wind was howling and they had to bend over almost double to protect themselves from the fierce stream of stinging sand. The wind howled and roared like some sort of wild beast. Ramose couldn't see any more than a cubit in front of him.

"Why don't we stop and wait for the wind to die down?" he shouted to Karoya.

"It's too dangerous," she yelled back. "If you sit still in a sandstorm, the sand will bury you. We have to keep moving. Just stay behind the camel."

Ramose shouted to Hapu. "Stay close." He grabbed his friends' hands and they bent into the wind.

Ramose lost all sense of time. He couldn't tell whether the sandstorm had been blowing for a

few minutes or for hours. He hung on tightly to
Hapu and Karoya's hands. Every now and again
he glanced up to make sure that he could still see
the camel's rump in front of him.

Suddenly, Karoya's hand was wrenched out of
his. He turned. Through the stream of flying sand
he saw that her legs had disappeared up to her
knees.

"It's a sand pool," she yelled. Her voice was
almost lost in the roar and screech of the wind.
"Soft sand. I'm sinking."

Ramose stumbled towards her.

"No! Don't come closer or you'll sink too,"
Karoya shouted. "Get Mery!"

The cat's basket was sitting on top of the soft
sand, too light to sink. Ramose reached out and
grabbed it. Karoya was sinking further into the
sand. In a few moments she would disappear
completely.

Ramose quickly took off the long garment that
he was wearing and, holding on to one end, threw
the other end to Karoya. She reached out for it,
but couldn't grab hold. The sharp sand bit into
Ramose's bare skin. It felt like a thousand scorpions were stinging him.

"Hapu," he shouted. "Hold on to my hand."

He could hardly see Karoya now. She was
struggling to clamber out of the soft sand, but the
more she struggled the further she sank into it.

With Hapu clinging onto his hand, Ramose edged towards the sand pool. He could feel his feet sink up to his ankles. He didn't dare go any further. He threw the coat towards Karoya again. She managed to grab hold of one of the sleeves. Ramose felt his legs disappear into the sand.

"Pull me back," he screamed at Hapu. "I'm sinking too."

He felt his friend grip him around the waist with both hands. Ramose held on to the hem of his coat. He felt the cloth give slightly and realised with horror that the stitching in the sleeve was breaking. He leaned out further, amazed that skinny little Hapu had found the strength to hold the weight of both Karoya and him. He hoped he could keep it up.

Ramose hauled in the garment hand over hand. The stitches kept breaking, until the sleeve was only attached to a couple of finger-widths of cloth. Ramose reached out and grasped hold of the sleeve just as the last stitch broke. He pulled the sleeve with all his might until he could see Karoya's fingers about to lose their grip. He grabbed her by the wrist. Once she felt him, she reached out with her other hand and grabbed hold of his arm with a grip like crocodile jaws. Ramose's strength was fading, but he knew he couldn't let his friend go. Using his arm like a rope, Karoya clawed her way to the edge of the sand pool and crawled back to firmer ground. All three collapsed exhausted onto the sand.

After a while the wind started to die down. The biting sand stopped blowing at them. The air finally cleared. They looked around.

"Where are the nomads?" said Hapu.

Ramose, worn out after so much exertion so soon after his sickness, didn't have the strength to move. Karoya struggled to the top of a dune. She turned in a circle, scanning the horizon in all directions.

"I can't see them anywhere."

Ramose crawled up the sand dune. He had to see for himself. Huge dunes stretched in every direction like a sheet of crumpled papyrus. He strained his eyes looking for a series of black shapes that would represent the nomads and their animals. All he could see was sand.

"They have to be out there somewhere," he said. "There hasn't been enough time for them to walk over the horizon."

"They're hidden by the dunes. Even if we did wait here until we caught sight of them, we wouldn't be able to catch up with them."

The sun was low in the sky. They were all dead tired after their ordeal. Ramose and Karoya crawled back down the dune and collapsed.

As the darkness crept around them, the three friends huddled together. Ramose closed his eyes.

He saw an image of the desert, nothing but sand in every direction as far as the eye could see. On the endless sand he could see three small black dots. That was them. They were lost, hopelessly lost. They had no food, and hardly any water. Ramose could think of nothing on earth that could save them. He prayed to Seth, who was also the god of the desert and foreign lands, not to abandon him and his friends.

"We could last for quite a while without food," Karoya said, as they sat in the growing light the following morning. "But without water, we haven't got a chance."

She shook their water-skin. It was less than a quarter full.

"Zeyd will come back and look for us, won't he?" Hapu asked hopefully.

Karoya stroked Mery and shook her head.

"He helped us before."

"He didn't change the path of his journey, though. Nomads have to keep moving to the next oasis. They couldn't risk the lives of their goats by stopping to look for us. Without the goats the nomads die."

They sat in silence as the sun rose in the sky.

Ramose sat up. He still felt very weak. "We should walk east, towards the Nile."

"The river must be many days march away,"

said Karoya. "We can't possibly reach it without food or water."

"I'd rather walk than sit and wait for death."

"Okay. We'll walk," said Hapu.

Karoya nodded. She sewed the sleeve back onto Ramose's nomad coat as best she could with a length of fishing line.

"I'm sorry," Ramose said. "Neither of you would be in this situation if it wasn't for me."

Ramose looked at his friends. Why had they chosen to take this journey with him? It was the duty of all Egyptians to serve the pharaoh and his family, but when Hapu started to help Ramose, he didn't even know he was the pharaoh's son. Karoya should have hated him. It was the pharaoh who was responsible for her being taken from her family and becoming a slave.

"You shouldn't have followed me, Hapu."

Hapu put his bag on his shoulder. "It's the will of the gods," he said.

"You could have gone to Tombos, Karoya. You would have been closer to your home. Why did you choose to come with me?"

Karoya shrugged. "You needed my help."

Ramose had hoped that when he became pharaoh, he would be able to reward his friends for their friendship. It didn't look like that was going to happen now.

Ramose turned towards the rising sun and

started to walk. Hapu followed him. Karoya picked up Mery's basket and set out after Hapu.

No one spoke. There was nothing to say. The sun beat down on them. It felt hotter than it had on the other days they'd spent in the desert. By mid-morning they had already drunk all the water. Ramose could think of nothing but how thirsty he was. He imagined large terracotta jars of water, pools and ponds; he remembered the Nile. He didn't look ahead, but just stared at the sand beneath him, and his feet making one point-less step after another. They trudged through the valleys between the huge mounds of sand, skirt-ing around dune after dune.

"Ramose," said Karoya behind him. Her voice sounded dry and crackly like a piece of burnt papyrus. "You've turned south. We aren't heading east any more."

Ramose looked up at the sun. It was directly above them. When the sun was in that position he found it hard to tell which way was which.

"What does it matter?" he said, continuing to walk in the same direction.

Karoya didn't argue. She followed in his foot-steps. Hapu's eyes were glazed over. Ramose had seen that look in animals that were close to death. He guessed his own eyes had the same look. Ramose kept walking.

The visions of water in Ramose's head grew

stronger. He remembered the jars and jars of water that the palace servants had poured over him day after day as they bathed him. He also remembered the lotus pool in the palace gardens. He pictured the irrigation canals in the Nile valley, recalling with envy the water poured on the rows of vegetables. He would have given anything for a cup of water, just the amount given to a single lettuce or onion plant. But he had nothing to give.

Images of his dear sister and Keneben, his tutor, drifted into his mind. The last time he had seen them was the day they had escaped from the high priest. The royal barge had sailed past them on its way to Thebes. Aboard it, Ramose had seen his beautiful sister, Princess Hatshepsut, and Keneben. He had thought Keneben was still banished in the distant land of Punt.

Ramose had also glimpsed his father on the barge. Pharaoh had looked unwell, but he was healthy enough to make the long river journey to Thebes. Ramose had splashed into the river waving and shouting, but they hadn't seen him. They didn't know where he was. They would never know what had happened to him. He had also seen his half-brother, the brat Prince Tuthmosis, and the boy's evil mother Queen Mutnofret.

When darkness fell, they collapsed in the sand.

When the sun rose, they struggled to their feet and walked again. They walked without thinking about which direction they were going in. They each stared down at their feet, as if a great deal of concentration was required to keep them moving. Their steps became slower and shorter, until they were merely shuffling through the sand a few finger-widths at a time.

Ramose looked up at the sky. The sun was lower. Was it morning or afternoon? He couldn't remember. Was this only the second day of walking? Surely it had been longer. He looked around him. The dunes had softened and become smaller and lower. Instead of walking around them, they walked in a straight line over them. It was easier than having to decide which valley to follow. Ramose stopped. Up ahead he saw something glint in the sunlight. It was a reflection of the blue sky.

"The devil's mirror," said Ramose hoarsely, pointing to the reflection.

Karoya looked to where he was pointing. She nodded. Her knees collapsed beneath her, as if the effort of nodding had taken all the energy she had. She slumped to the ground. Hapu collapsed next to her. Ramose kept his eyes on the bright glint of reflected light. This mirage was more detailed than the ones he'd seen before. He could actually see faint images of palm fronds. Ramose thought it must be the effects of lack of water. He stumbled a few more steps. The reflection disappeared, but the image of the palm tree grew clearer.

"I must be close to death," he whispered, though the words couldn't get out of his parched mouth. "I'm seeing things."

He shuffled up the gentle slope of the next sand dune, but his legs crumpled beneath him. He crawled on his hands and knees, as the palm fronds in front of him multiplied and tamarisks appeared as well. Suddenly, the sand beneath him sprouted tufts of dry grass. He crawled to the top of the dune. A green valley stretched before him. A forest of date palms, tamarisks and acacia trees sprung from the ground. In the middle of the trees was a pool of water, perfectly reflecting the sky. Ramose stared.

He croaked out a call to his friends. They struggled to their feet and made their way very slowly to the top of the shallow dune. They blinked as they stared at the brilliant vision of green and blue—colours they hadn't seen for days and days.

"Is it real?" Hapu's voice was a hoarse whisper, "or have we passed into the underworld?"

Ramose stood up and took a few steps towards the trees and the pool. They didn't edge further away as he approached, as the heat haze had.

Instead they grew closer. He could see that the palms were laden with dates. Ramose found a last reserve of energy and ran towards the pool. He splashed into the water and then fell full length. The coolness of the water took his breath away. He gulped in mouthfuls of it.

"It's real," he spluttered.

4

ORACLE OF THE OASIS

KAROYA AND HAPU approached the pool more cautiously. Karoya dipped her fingers into the water and scooped up a handful. She drank it and then sank to her knees to drink more. Hapu stood ankle-deep in the water and cried.

"I don't understand how there can be a pool of water in the middle of the desert," Hapu said, after they had drunk their fill. The water had a bitter, salty taste, but no one was complaining. They were sitting in the shade of a tamarisk tree chewing on the dried-up dates that had fallen on the ground. No one had the strength yet to climb one of the palms for the fresher fruit.

"It's an oasis," said Ramose.

"Without them nomads wouldn't be able to survive," said Karoya.

"But where does the water come from?" asked Hapu, still puzzled.

"It comes up from the great invisible river that runs beneath the earth," replied Karoya.

Hapu shook his head in disbelief. "It's like magic."

Ramose didn't want to spoil his friends' good mood, but he was already thinking of what lay ahead of them.

"The Nile is still many, many cubits away and we only have one small water-skin and nothing but dates to eat."

"We can live here for a long time," said Karoya. "There will be snakes, birds, frogs. We can find things to eat."

"And stay here until we grow old?" Hapu didn't like the idea.

"No," replied Karoya. "We will wait until the next nomads arrive."

"That could be ages."

"It might be months, yes. Do you have a better idea?"

Hapu didn't.

The sun was low in the sky.

"It will be getting cold soon," said Karoya. "We need to collect fuel to make a fire."

The three friends walked around the oasis collecting dead palm fronds and dry grass.

"Look what I've found," shouted Karoya. She picked up a dead branch that had fallen from one of the tamarisk trees. "We'll be able to have a good fire tonight."

Wood was very precious in Egypt and they wouldn't have dreamt of wasting it in a fire normally, but out in the desert it didn't seem to matter.

Karoya arranged some stones to make a fireplace. She laid a pile of grass and palm leaves in the fireplace and then she got out her fire-making tools. These consisted of three pieces of wood: a flat stick with a well dug into it, a smooth rod and a stick with a length of gut tied at each end like a small bow. She wrapped the string of the bow around the rod and placed the end of the rod in the well in the flat stick. Then she started pulling the bow back and forth so that the upright stick twirled at great speed. Hapu laid small pieces of dry grass near the well, waiting for the wood to get hot enough to burn the grass. Ramose picked up the dead tree branch and broke it across his knee. The crack echoed in the silence. A shrill sound suddenly came out of the trees.

"Eigh! Eigh! Eigh!"

The friends all spun round. Hapu screamed in terror. A small dark creature, covered from head to toe in black rags, appeared from among the trees. It was wielding a heavy stick. The creature ran straight at Ramose, knocked him to the ground and started hitting him with the stick.

"It's a demon," yelled Hapu.

Karoya rushed at the demon, trying to rescue her friend.

"Stop!" she shouted.

The creature turned with a whirl of tattered rags and set upon Karoya, scratching her with long, curved claws and growling like a tiger. Ramose jumped to his feet and grabbed the demon, pinning its arms behind its back. He was surprised at how easy it was. The creature's arms were thin and frail. He pulled back the black rags wrapped around its head to get a better look at their attacker. To his surprise, he discovered it was an old woman—an ancient woman. She had a tangle of grey hair, milky-white eyes and a dark-brown face that was wrinkled like an old leather bag. She screamed out horrible sounds and feebly tried to escape from Ramose's grasp.

"It must be the spirit of someone who died in

the desert?" said Hapu, looking at her fearfully.

"I don't think spirits can bash people," said Ramose, rubbing the bump on his head.

"Where did she come from?" asked Karoya, peering around in the growing darkness. "There's no one else here."

"Where are your people?" Ramose asked the old woman. "Where are you from?"

The woman didn't seem to understand him. Hapu waved his hand in front of her eyes.

"I think she's blind," he said.

"I'll keep an eye on her," said Ramose. "You two see if you can find something to eat."

Since their last meal with the nomads two days before, they'd had nothing to eat but a few dried dates.

"Hapu, can you climb up one of these palms and get some dates?"

Hapu nodded and started to climb a date palm.

"Dates," said the old woman in an angry voice. "My dates."

The three friends stared at the wrinkled face. She had spoken in Egyptian.

"We're hungry," said Karoya slowly. "Very hungry."

The old woman's brow wrinkled even more than it was already. She reached up and touched Karoya's face.

"Children!" she exclaimed. She spoke with a

heavy accent, and the word came slowly as if she was searching in a part of her mind she hadn't used for a long time. "Come!" she said. "Come!"

The woman led Karoya by the hand. It was almost dark now, but the old woman walked confidently through the trees as if it were broad daylight. Ramose and Hapu looked at each other, and then followed her.

"I thought she was blind," whispered Hapu.

"She is, but she must know the oasis very well."

The woman led them away from the pool and through the grove of trees to a rocky outcrop. There was a fireplace with a fire smouldering in it. A piece of dark material, similar to the nomads' tents, hung from a rock overhang. It was held in place by stones. The woman must have slept behind this rough curtain. There were cooking pots and baskets. Tethered nearby were three goats.

"It looks like she's lived here for a long time," said Ramose.

The woman made them sit down. There was a cooking pot on the fire. Something was simmering inside it—something that smelled like meat cooking. Such delicious smells had seemed unimaginable half an hour ago. The woman made bread from flour. She gave them each a gourd bowl and filled them to the brim with the goat stew. They ate ravenously.

"It tastes wonderful," said Hapu, gratefully.

While they were eating, the old woman made sweet cakes with honey and dates. They ate them, still hot, with fresh goats' milk. It was a feast.

"I think this is all a mirage," said Ramose, swallowing another cake. "Like the heat haze pools we saw out in the desert."

"Yes, but we couldn't get near them," said Hapu, draining his bowl of milk. "This isn't moving away."

An angry miaow came from Karoya's basket. Karoya leapt up to open it.

"I forgot about Mery!" she said, letting the cat out. "Poor Mery, you're hungry too, aren't you?"

Mery wailed miserably. The old woman jumped at the sound. Karoya put down her bowl of milk and let the cat drink. Mery purred. The old woman was puzzled by the sound. She cocked her ear to listen more closely.

"It's a cat," Karoya replied. "It's my pet."

The old woman had heard of cats, but thought they were imaginary beasts like griffins and camels. Ramose smiled to himself, remembering the camel. Karoya guided the woman's hand so that it stroked Mery's fur. The old woman's grim little mouth broke into a smile.

"Warm," she said. "Soft."

Now that the friends had eaten their fill and

were warmed by the fire, they began to relax. The old woman, speaking slowly in a half-forgotten language, told them her story.

They discovered that her name was Jenu. When she was a young girl, her father had been the chief of a nomad tribe, just like the one they had travelled with.

"One day we went to Kharga, an oasis so big it takes a week to walk from one end to the other," she told them. "Egyptians were there, building their temples. They took away all the young people for slaves." Jenu shook her head sorrowfully. "I lived for many years as a slave in the house of an Egyptian."

When her eyesight started to fail, her master didn't want to feed a blind slave. She was taken to the edge of the desert and left there; told to return to her tribe. Of course, she had no idea where her people would be. She wandered for many days and was close to death when a tribe of nomads came across her. It had been a bad year in the desert and the nomads had lost many of their goats. They could not take on another mouth to feed. Instead, they brought her to the oasis, gave her some food and left her there when they moved on. If the gods will it, you will survive, they had said.

"And the gods did will it," said the old woman. "May they be praised forever."

After the food ran out, Jenu had lived on dates and frogs. Then other nomads came to the oasis and each tribe gave her a little of what they had.

"I give them something in return," said Jenu.

"What?" asked Ramose. "What do you have to give?"

She told them how, as her vision of the world had disappeared, she had discovered an inner vision was growing in its place.

"The gods, in their wisdom, have made me an oracle," she said. "I can read people's futures."

Stories of the Oracle of the Oasis had spread among the nomads. Now, whenever they visited the oasis, they asked Jenu to look into their future.

Ramose and his friends sat wide-eyed listening to Jenu's story, forgetting their exhaustion.

"Can you see everyone's future?" asked Hapu.

Jenu shook her head. "Only those who the gods favour." She reached out and found Ramose's hand. "She will lift the mists on your future."

The old woman wouldn't say anything else and disappeared into her tent, telling them she was tired.

The following morning the friends awoke to find Jenu making breakfast. After they had eaten fresh bread, goats' cheese and dried figs, they explored the oasis. It was quite small, perhaps a thousand cubits from one end to the other. Ramose remembered courtyards in the palace that were bigger.

As well as the tethered goats, Jenu had a small garden where she grew a patch of wheat, some herbs and onions. Other food, gifts from nomads, was stored in jars and baskets. Nomads had been there only two weeks earlier, so her stores were full.

Jenu had a list of things that she wanted her visitors to do for her. Her simple weaving loom had broken and she wanted them to mend it for her. She wanted someone to climb the trees and knock down fresh dates. The sharp-edged stone that she used for cutting had shattered and she needed a new one.

The oasis was a pleasant place. Karoya and Hapu spent the whole day helping the old woman. Mery skipped around, attacking tufts of grass and chasing birds, delighted that she was no longer squashed in her basket. Jenu was enjoying the company of her young guests. She no longer looked like a frightening old witch. Overnight she had transformed into a smiling grandmother.

Ramose busied himself around the oasis, but he wasn't laughing and chattering like the others. He was thinking about what the old woman had said the night before. Could she really see into his future? If she could, did he want to know what she saw?

In the evening, after a filling meal of tasty goat stew, Karoya and Hapu sat around Jenu's cooking fire as if they hadn't a problem in the world. Jenu sat spinning goat hair into thread, twirling it with her fingers. Hapu told funny stories that made the old woman laugh. Karoya mended Jenu's tattered tent cloth. Mery lay with her stomach towards the fire. Ramose sat to one side, poking at the fire. He knew that his problems weren't over yet.

"Jenu, do you know how far it is to the river?" he asked.

The others fell silent.

"A long way," said the old woman.

"How many days on foot?" Ramose asked.

"Many days," replied the old woman.

Ramose could tell she was being unhelpful on purpose. He knew he had to ask her the question he had been avoiding. He poked at the embers of the fire, sending out sparks that singed Mery's fur and made her leap up. The cat settled down again, this time in Jenu's lap. Mery had grown fond of the old woman who gave her milk and meat.

"Jenu," said Ramose at last. "Can you see my future?"

She beckoned Ramose. He got up and sat next

to the old woman. She took his hand in hers. He could feel the calluses on her palms. Her long, claw-like fingernails scraped his skin. Her face changed. The smiling grandmother face disappeared and was replaced by a stern-faced mask. Jenu's white unseeing eyes changed too. They lost their sightless look and Ramose felt as if she could see right into his soul. A single gust of wind arose out of the perfectly still night. A distant hyena chose that moment to howl.

"Some things I see. Others are unclear."

"Tell me what you see."

"You must give me something first. Something dear to you."

Ramose reached for his bag. He only had one thing to give. He pulled out his heart scarab, stroked its cool surface and put the blue jewel in Jenu's hand.

The old woman felt the stone with her crooked fingers and shook her head.

"Not this," she said. "I have no need of this."

"But it's the only thing of value I have," Ramose said.

"You have to give something that I need," replied the old woman.

"You seem to have all you need. I have nothing else to give you."

The old woman's white eyes narrowed. "You have friendship."

"If you want my friendship, you have it already," said Ramose.

The old woman shook her head. "But you will leave and I will only have the memory of friendship."

"Are you saying you want me to stay?" asked Ramose.

"Not you. You have a journey to finish. You have friends. I have no one."

Ramose looked at Karoya and Hapu in alarm, finally understanding what the old woman wanted. They were staring back at him wide-eyed.

"I can't give you my friends," said Ramose. "They aren't mine to give."

"The slave girl is yours to give, if you choose."

"No," Ramose cried, his voice rising in fear and anger. "I don't own her. She's free to go wherever she wishes."

"Is she?"

Ramose knew that Karoya was actually the pharaoh's property.

"She is useful to you now," continued Jenu. "But if you find what you are seeking, then what will become of her?"

"I'll take care of her." Ramose snatched his hand away. "I've changed my mind. I don't want to know my future."

"The choice is yours," said Jenu.

"Why can't you just tell him?" asked Hapu.

"It is the way of the oracle. She will not see clearly unless Ramose gives me something of his that I need."

Mery stirred in the old woman's lap. The cat stood up, turned around twice then settled down again.

"What about Mery?" asked Karoya.

"No, Karoya," said Ramose. "Mery is yours. Jenu wants something of mine."

Karoya turned to the old woman. "Would the cat be a suitable gift?" she asked. "She is a good friend."

The old woman thought for a moment and then nodded.

"I don't want to hear about my future," said Ramose angrily. "I don't believe in oracles. I know what I have to do. I don't need an oracle to tell me."

"The oracle's knowledge is important," said the old woman. "Without it you might fail."

"I give Mery to you, Ramose," said Karoya. Mery slept in the old woman's lap, unaware that she was the centre of attention. "She is yours now."

"No!"

"The gods have brought us here, Ramose," said Hapu. "Perhaps it was for a reason. Listen to what Jenu has to say."

"Let her tell your future instead," Ramose said. "Or yours, Karoya."

"No, Ramose," said Karoya. "My future has been bound with yours since I chose to follow you and not go where the pharaoh sent me. Take Mery. I give her to you."

Ramose looked from Karoya to the old woman.

"Are you sure, Karoya?"

"I'm sure."

"Will you give the cat to me, Ramose?" asked the old woman.

Ramose nodded. "Yes."

"The oracle accepts your gift," said Jenu. She spoke as if the oracle was another person.

The old woman reached out for Ramose's hand again. Ramose glared at the old woman, but placed his hand in hers.

"Ask the oracle what you want to know."

There was so much he wanted to know, Ramose hardly knew where to begin. "Will I see my father again before he dies?"

"Yes."

"Will I achieve my goal?"

"Yes."

"Will I—"

"You can ask only one more question of the oracle."

"Why didn't you say that before?" snapped Ramose. "This isn't a game."

"The oracle doesn't like to give up her knowledge."

Ramose had so many questions. If he were to become the pharaoh, would he be happy? Would he be a good pharaoh? Would Vizier Wersu still want him dead? Ramose thought for a moment. He had to word his last question carefully.

"Does the oracle see anything in my future that I need to know?"

The old woman smiled a small, grim smile. "The oracle has a warning for you."

"What is it?"

"The blue lotus can hide a bee in its petals."

Ramose opened his mouth to say something. The old woman held up her hand to stop him.

"A perfect jewel will stay buried in the earth, yet the maid at the millstone holds it out in her hand."

Jenu still held her hand in the air.

"Trust the crocodile and bow down before the frog."

Ramose waited, expecting more. But the hard mask of the old woman's face melted away and she changed back into a smiling grandmother again.

"Is that it?" Ramose cried.

Jenu nodded. "The oracle's words are truth." She looked limp and drained.

"But, they're just riddles. What do they mean?"

"That's for you to discover. The oracle has been generous. She doesn't often say so much."

Ramose felt cheated, as if the old woman had tricked him. He took his reed mat and unrolled it away from the others. He curled up in the smelly goat-hair coat that the nomads had given him. He didn't want to speak to anybody.

5

ABYDOS

T HE NEXT DAY, Ramose woke with a sense of urgency. He had dreamt he'd seen his father walking in the palace gardens. In the dream Ramose had called out to him, but Pharaoh couldn't hear him. Ramose had tried to get closer to him, but whichever way he turned there was a wall or a pond or a row of tall plants in his way. Ramose knew he had to leave the oasis. He had delayed for too long. "I'm walking to Thebes," he told his friends. "I have to leave immediately."

"You don't know how far it is to the river," said Karoya. "You may not be able to carry enough food and water to get you there.'

"It's too risky," complained Hapu.

"I have to go," said Ramose. "You two stay here and wait for the next nomads to come along."

Ramose didn't like to admit it, but the oracle's words had affected him strongly. He still didn't know what they meant, but whatever his destiny was, he had to face it. He had wandered from his path. He had wasted valuable time. He had to get to Thebes as soon as possible. He had to see his father.

He asked Jenu if he could have some leather for a water-skin. She nodded and cut him a length of goat hide from her stock. She showed him how to make the bag with the hairy side facing in. She also gave him a supply of dried goat meat and cheese. Ramose mended his sandals and his nomad coat. By the time he had finished his preparations, it was too late in the day to start his journey.

"We're not staying behind," said Karoya as the sun started to get low in the sky. "We're coming with you."

"You don't have to," said Ramose. "Stay here."

"And then what would we do?" asked Hapu.

Ramose looked at his friends. Since the day they had chosen to follow him instead of going to the place that had been allotted to them, their destinies were tied up with his.

Hapu looked at the pool of water unhappily. "I think it would be better if we all waited here until other nomads come. But if you want to leave now, I'll come too."

"I'll be grateful for your company."

They left before sunrise the next morning. Jenu bade them all goodbye.

"The gods will be with you," said the old woman. "They won't abandon you."

Karoya said goodbye to Mery with tears in her eyes. Jenu clutched Mery to her in case she tried to follow them.

"The cat will keep me warm at night," Jenu said happily.

Earlier, Ramose had offered to come back and give her as much gold as she wanted once he had achieved his goal, if she gave the cat back. The old woman had refused.

The three friends loaded themselves up with food and water and walked out into the desert. The sun rose in front of them. They walked towards it in single file, keeping space between them. No one felt like talking.

In the heat of midday, they stopped and made a shelter from the hot sun with a length of goat-hair cloth and some sticks that Jenu had given them. They ate a light meal, drank a little water and slept until the worst of the heat had passed.

When they woke, they walked until two or three hours after the sun had set, then ate cold meat and cheese. They slept again and then walked in the darkness before dawn. They spoke little, not wanting to waste precious energy on idle talk.

Ramose wasn't sure that they would make it to the river. He wasn't convinced that he had a future just because a blind nomad woman had told him so. He kept walking.

Ramose glanced at Karoya. She had hardly spoken since they had left the oasis. Once or twice he had seen her wipe away some tears. He knew what a great sacrifice she had made for him. Karoya loved Mery dearly. The cat had been the only thing that was truly hers and she had given it away for his sake. All he'd got in return for her sacrifice were a few meaningless words from the oracle. He hoped one day he'd be able to repay her.

The routine was the same the next day and the next. Ramose didn't tire; he just grew stronger and stronger. He began to feel like the desert would never stop and that didn't matter because he knew he could walk forever. He was very surprised, therefore, when at mid-morning on the fifth day a large temple gradually rose up over the horizon, bright and shimmering in the heat haze. He recognised it immediately. It was a place he had visited before.

Abydos was a big town, not as big as Thebes, but big nonetheless. It had sprung up around the Temple of Osiris. The people who lived in the town all worked at the temple. Those who didn't have jobs within the temple buildings worked outside the walls producing food for the workers and for offerings to Osiris.

"We shouldn't have come into the town," hissed Karoya.

"We had to. We've run out of food."

Ramose hoped that in such a big town they might not attract as much attention as they had in the villages along the Nile. He was wrong. He hadn't realised how foreign they looked. They were still wearing the heavy clothing made from dark, hairy cloth given to them by the nomads. They hadn't bathed properly in weeks. Ramose had no idea what his hair looked like, but Hapu's was a tangled mess.

The temple workers in their white linen kilts and tunics looked spotlessly clean. They all smelled of perfumed oils and incense. Everyone who passed Ramose and his friends stepped around them so that they didn't get too close to the foul-smelling foreigners.

"What are we going to do?" said Ramose. "We have no gold for food. We can't beg on the streets."

They wandered through Abydos, past the neat houses of the temple workers. Wherever they went, people turned to stare at them. They walked through the metalworkers' quarter. The sound of hammers and bellows stopped as they passed. It was the same as they walked through the part of the town where the potters worked. The potters' wheels stopped turning and all eyes followed the strangers.

"We'll get arrested," said Hapu.

"What for? We haven't done anything wrong," said Ramose.

"Not recently," said Hapu.

"Egyptians don't like strangers," said Karoya. "People will want to know who we are. What are you going to tell them?"

"I'll think of something," Ramose answered.

Hapu and Karoya looked at Ramose doubtfully. Ramose actually didn't have any ideas for a cover story. He was tired of sneaking and hiding, tired of hiding from his enemies. He was ready to face them—the sooner the better. He just had to work out how to go about it.

They found themselves at the foot of the temple walls. The dazzling white walls loomed above them.

"What is your business in Abydos?" demanded a stern voice behind them.

The three friends turned. A man in a perfectly white kilt without a crease stood glaring at them. He had a shaved head which shone in the sunlight. His eyebrows and eyelashes had also been removed. This told Ramose that the man was a priest.

"I'm a scribe," said Ramose, not knowing what else to say.

The priest was puzzled. From the stranger's clothing, he was probably expecting Ramose to have the harsh tones and ugly accent of a foreigner. Yet Ramose spoke in perfect Egyptian with the grammar of a scholar.

"You can't be the scribe we're expecting," said the puzzled priest. "You're far too young."

The priest was waiting for an answer. Ramose didn't know what to say.

"No, he's not," Hapu said, suddenly. "The scribe had an unfortunate accident."

Ramose and Karoya looked across at Hapu in surprise.

"Yes," continued Hapu, "the scribe's right hand was crushed when a block of stone fell from a sled."

"How unfortunate," said the priest, still frowning dubiously at the strangers.

"This is the scribe's apprentice," said Hapu.

The priest looked at Ramose's nomad coat and his worn sandals.

"I am not at all sure that an apprentice can take the role of temple scribe," he said, scratching his shaved head.

Hapu thought for a moment. "He was an apprentice," he said. "But now he isn't. His training is finished."

The priest peered at Ramose again. Ramose thought that after his recent adventures he must look at least five years older than he actually was.

"He is the cleverest apprentice in memory," said Hapu, who seemed to be enjoying inventing a new history for Ramose as much as he enjoyed making up stories as they travelled. "The scribe is completely confident that Ramose is skilled enough to take his place."

The priest looked at Hapu. "And you are..."

"I," said Hapu, pulling himself to his full height of almost three cubits, "I am Hapu, temple artist and assistant to scribe Ramose."

The priest was still troubled by the strange clothing of the scribe and his party. "Where are you from? Somewhere in the south, beyond the cataracts?"

"We have come from Kharga Oasis," continued Hapu. "We were attacked by barbarians on the way. They took all our possessions, even our clothes, and abandoned us in the desert. We're lucky we survived."

"What were you doing in Kharga Oasis?" asked the priest, looking terrified at the thought of being lost in the desert. "I thought you were coming from Thebes."

"Scribe Ramose had to record some details about a new temple at the oasis," Hapu told him. "We were attacked as we were returning to the Nile."

"How terrible. What else can you expect from barbarians, though?" the priest said shaking his head.

While he was out in the desert, Ramose had vowed that when he became pharaoh he would tell Egyptians that nomads were not criminals and barbarians. He'd only been back in Egypt for a few hours and already he had broken his promise and was confirming the same old myths and lies.

"How did you get from Kharga to Abydos?" asked the wide-eyed priest, who, like most Egyptians, would rather have jumped into a pit of snakes than venture into the desert for any reason.

"We walked," said Ramose simply.

"Praise Amun for protecting you," said the horrified priest.

"We are very tired and hungry," said Hapu.

"Perhaps you could show us to our quarters and arrange for our servant to fetch us some food."

Karoya glared at Hapu.

"Yes, immediately," replied the priest.

The priest led them towards the first pylon of the temple of Osiris. The pylon, a gateway flanked on either side by huge tapering stone towers, was covered with carved images and hieroglyphs. They didn't enter the temple though. Instead of walking through the pylon, the priest led them around the eastern wall of the temple to a group of simpler, lower buildings where the temple craftsmen lived. They entered one of the houses. Inside it was cool and clean.

"We will need clothes," Hapu said.

The priest nodded.

"Scribe Ramose will require scribal tools, since his own were stolen," said Hapu.

The priest looked at Ramose to confirm this. Ramose nodded and smiled weakly. He was beginning to wonder what Hapu was getting them into.

"If your slave girl will follow me," the priest said. "I will provide her with all that you need."

Karoya followed the priest.

"Now what do we do?" asked Ramose, once the priest was out of sight.

"I don't know. I thought you had a plan."

"I do. I have to get to Thebes to see my father."

"And how did you imagine you would do that?" Ramose hesitated. "I don't know."

"Well, it's time you thought about that," said Hapu. "Staying in Abydos for a while will give you some time to work out the best way to get to Thebes."

"Or it will give me some time to get thrown into prison for pretending to be someone who I'm not."

"You told him you were a scribe," said Hapu, defensively. "I just…added a few details."

Servants arrived with terracotta jars of water for bathing. Others followed with food—the sort of food they hadn't seen for months: grapes and watermelon; freshly baked pyramid-shaped loaves of bread; lentils flavoured with cumin; roast goose and a salad of lettuce, cucumber and spring onions.

Karoya returned with clean clothes. Although they were all hungry, they were eager to wash off the dirt and sweat from their long journey. Once they were clean and wearing soft linen garments, they ate the food.

Ramose was glad to be dressed in Egyptian clothes again. And he was pleased to be full of good food, but Hapu was right. He didn't have a real plan. Now that he was getting closer to Thebes he began to wonder what exactly he was going to do.

"I have to think of a way to get inside the

palace," Ramose said. "I have to see my father without the vizier knowing."

"You'll need a disguise," said Hapu.

"I'm too tired to think of anything now," said Ramose. "We'll devise a plan in the morning."

"I will sleep outside, like a good slave," said Karoya.

Ramose smiled at her. "I am very glad that you are both here to help me."

Hapu unrolled his reed mat on the floor. Ramose slept on a comfortable bed with a roof over his head for the first time since he had been whisked away from the palace. It felt strange.

The next morning, Ramose was woken by Karoya bringing in breakfast. Hapu yawned and stretched and surveyed the platters of food with pleasure.

"Can't we just stay here in Abydos?" he asked, helping himself to some plum cakes.

Ramose picked up a fig and walked out into the courtyard. The morning air was already hot. He didn't like Abydos. It was a dry desert town, too far away from the river. He was just about to bite into the fig when the priest who had spoken to them the day before arrived. He handed a pen box and a palette to Ramose.

"You are to work at the Temple of Osiris," the priest said. "I will take you there."

"What, now?" asked Hapu, through a mouthful of cake.

"Yes," said the priest. "The work has been delayed for far too long already. It must be completed in time for the Festival of Osiris next month. Come."

The priest turned and marched off. Ramose and Hapu had no choice but to follow him. He led them to the pylon. Guards allowed the priest to enter. They walked through the huge gateway. Through the pylon, they found themselves on a long avenue lined on either side with enormous sphinxes made of red granite.

The avenue led to the second pylon. They passed through this gateway and finally entered the temple itself. Inside it was cool and dimly lit by small windows high above their heads.

Temple workers were busy going about the daily business of the temple. Young women passed by carrying baskets of food-offerings on their heads. The sound of chanting and the smell of burning incense drifted from chambers that they passed.

The ancient temple of Osiris was being repaired. Ramose had to record the progress of the work and ensure that the architect's instructions were followed.

After half a day of writing out the texts to be carved on the walls in hieroglyphs, Ramose looked at his ink-stained hands and threw down his reed pen.

"I can't stay here," he said to Hapu, who was managing to look busy while doing nothing at all. "I have to get to Thebes. I have to see my father."

"What are you going to do, run to Thebes?" said Hapu. "If we work here for a while, we'll earn grain which we can exchange for passage on a boat."

"It will be too late by then, I know it," said Ramose. "I'll go to the river and stow away on a boat."

"I don't think that's a good idea," said Hapu.

Ramose was already on his way out of the temple, though. Hapu hurried after him. The guards at the temple gate glared at them suspiciously as they passed. Ramose headed back to the house where they were staying. Karoya was kneading dough.

"What are you doing back so early?"

"We're leaving," said Ramose.

"But—"

"We're leaving now."

Karoya didn't argue further. She put her kneading stone in her bag. She wrapped the bread dough in a cloth and put that in the bag as well.

"Leave the nomad coats," said Ramose picking up his reed bag. "We don't want to look like we're leaving. We have to pretend we're going to a job outside of the city."

Ramose strode down the street with his pen box and a piece of papyrus in his hand. "Don't look so guilty, Hapu. Pretend it's a game."

Hapu changed his expression from that of a guilty thief to that of a rich and haughty merchant. Ramose laughed at his friend. He was still smiling when they reached the edge of the city, walked out of the gate and found two temple guards waiting for them. One of the guards grabbed Ramose. The other one held Hapu and Karoya.

"What are you doing?" shouted Hapu, though he had a good idea.

The priest came out of the shadows of the city wall. One of the guards took Ramose's pen and papyrus. The other guard pulled the dough from Karoya's bag.

"You are under arrest for stealing temple property," the priest said.

"I knew we'd end up in prison," moaned Hapu.

They weren't taken to prison, though. The priest led them back to the temple and set them to work again, this time with the two guards watching them.

"You will work under guard until the work is finished," the priest said. "Then we will decide what to do with you."

Ramose had no choice. He picked up his pen and went back to work.

"We'll never get out of Abydos," he said miserably as they walked under guard back to their quarters that evening. "It'll take me a month to finish the work and then who knows what they'll do with me."

"Something will turn up," said Hapu hopefully.

When they got back to the house where they were staying, the priest was waiting for them.

"Now what's wrong?" said Hapu. "Did Ramose make a mistake with one of the hieroglyphs?"

"You are under arrest," said the priest.

"You don't have to remind me," said Ramose angrily. "I haven't forgotten that you arrested me this afternoon."

"There are new charges against you," replied the priest.

"What?" asked Ramose with a growing sense of dread.

"You are charged with impersonating a temple scribe," the priest said. "Guards, take them to the high priest."

The high priest was seated on a high-backed chair which was placed on a raised platform. He had a slender sceptre in one hand. Draped over his left shoulder was a leopard skin. The animal's head was still attached. Its dead eyes seemed to stare straight at Ramose.

The guards forced the boys to their knees. The high priest stood up and walked over to them, looking at them with distaste. "Which one is the impostor?" he asked.

One of the guards pointed to Ramose.

"He's not an impostor," said Hapu. "He's a replacement. We told you, the scribe was injured."

"Really?" said the high priest circling around the pair like a vulture. "I don't believe that a grubby wretch who wanders in from the desert is a temple scribe."

"Are you suggesting we're lying?" said Hapu, who was offended that his story wasn't believed, even though not a word of it was true.

"Yes, I am," replied the high priest. "We received a letter from the vizier last week. He is searching for three young people."

Ramose went cold. A few weeks in the desert didn't mean they were out of the vizier's clutches.

"That doesn't mean it's us," said Hapu, not sounding quite as bold.

"Unfortunately for you, the real scribe arrived this morning," said the priest. "He says he knows nothing about a replacement."

Hapu's confidence evaporated like water in the midday sun. "But, there must be a misunderstanding," he stammered.

"We'll see. Here is the scribe."

A man wearing a travel cloak entered the chamber. Ramose couldn't believe his eyes.

"Keneben!" he exclaimed.

6

HOMECOMING PRINCE

KENEBEN'S MOUTH fell open as he stared in amazement at Ramose. Then he broke into a smile. Ramose couldn't help himself. He rushed up to his tutor and threw his arms around him.

"My heart rejoices to see you," he said, unable to prevent tears blurring his vision.

Ramose owed his life to the tutor. It was

Keneben who had saved him from the queen's plot to kill him. His friend had then been banished to a foreign country.

"Are you well, Keneben?"

"Praise Amun, I live, prosper and have health."

The high priest watched this display of affection with complete surprise.

"This young man claims to be a scribe, taking your place. Is this true?"

"Not exactly, High Priest," said Keneben.

Ramose's smile faded.

"I come bearing news that the young scribe is unaware of." Keneben looked at Ramose, rustling a papyrus he was holding in his hand. "I have just received news from Thebes that will bring sorrow to us all."

Keneben paused.

"Our pharaoh is gravely ill. It is expected that he will ascend to heaven before the new moon."

"May Amun grant Pharaoh long life and happiness," said Ramose.

The high priest muttered similar words. It was what all Egyptians said whenever the pharaoh's name was mentioned, but no one meant it more sincerely than Ramose. The gods had granted his wish to see his tutor again. He hoped they would answer this prayer as well.

"Though I was about to start work here at Abydos," continued Keneben, "my services are urgently required at Thebes. Those of the young scribe will be required as well."

The high priest scowled as if he were disappointed that he couldn't punish Ramose.

"For this reason, High Priest, I ask your permission that we both return to Thebes as soon as possible."

"I will arrange for your passage to Thebes."

"Thank you, High Priest."

Keneben and Ramose bowed to the high priest and left.

"Is it true, Keneben?" asked Ramose when he and Keneben were alone. "Is my father really about to die?"

"It is true, Highness," said Keneben. "I wish it were happier circumstances that had brought us together."

Ramose took his tutor's hand in his. The last time he had spoken to Keneben was at the beginning of his adventures. He had said a sorrowful goodbye to his tutor as he left Thebes to start a life in exile as an apprentice scribe.

It seemed such a long time ago, but it was not much more than a year. He hadn't heard anything from his tutor since the secret letter he'd received at the Great Place, telling him that Keneben had been banished from the palace to the distant land of Punt. The tutor's skin was darker, as if he had spent a lot of time in harsh sun. There were lines on his face where before there had been none.

Keneben listened as Ramose told him all about his adventures since they had last met.

"I used to hate studying," said Ramose, "but there have been many times in the past months that I would have done anything to be back in the schoolroom copying texts."

"It has been difficult for you, Highness," said Keneben. "No prince should have to endure such hardship."

"What about you, Keneben?" Ramose asked.

"I worked as a scribe in Punt for many months," Keneben told him. "It was a most unhappy time."

"But now you've returned," said Ramose. "I saw you on the royal barge a few weeks ago. I knew that you were back from Punt and in favour with my sister again."

Keneben's grim mouth melted into a smile. "Yes. It was thanks to the efforts of your sister, Princess Hatshepsut, that I was able to return to the palace. She told the vizier that her studies were not progressing with the new tutor they had employed. She insisted that I teach her. I have been back at the palace now for several months."

The tutor's face flushed as he spoke of the princess. She had always had that effect on him.

They talked until late that evening. Ramose was unwilling to let Keneben out of his sight in case he disappeared again. It was a long time since he'd had news from the palace. He heard how his sister had grown tall and slender, how she had become even more beautiful, how her penmanship was the best Keneben had seen.

For Ramose, the palace had been a fading memory. There had been blank spaces in his memories, people and places that he could no longer picture. Now he could picture it all in detail. For the first time in months he felt like a prince again. It actually seemed possible that he would return to the palace and take his rightful place as the pharaoh's heir. He didn't want to lose that feeling.

Hapu and Karoya were asleep by the time Ramose went back to his quarters. He couldn't get to sleep. The air in the room was stifling. Eventually he climbed over the snoring Hapu and took his mattress out into the courtyard. He breathed in the cooler air and looked up at the stars. In a few days, he would be looking at the same stars from Thebes.

When he finally fell asleep, he dreamt about the riverbank at the edge of the palace gardens. There was one place where blue lotuses grew at the water's edge. In the dream, he was wading in the river, smelling the perfume of the lotus flowers. The sun was setting. He was thinking that this was strange, because the blue lotus flowers only opened in the morning. By evening they were usually closed tight. Then he looked again. The lotus petals turned into teeth and he realised he wasn't surrounded by lotus flowers but by crocodiles that were snapping at his legs.

The next day, Ramose, Hapu and Karoya were aboard a boat on their way to Thebes with Keneben. The boat was crowded with all sorts of people who were needed in Thebes. The death of a pharaoh was one of the most important events that could happen in Egypt. Though everyone prayed Pharaoh would live, preparations had to be made in case he didn't.

A strong breeze filled the sail. Ramose stood at the prow of the boat. He breathed in the cool Nile air. After travelling for so long on foot, it was wonderful to watch the fields and villages slip by so quickly. In a few days they would be in Thebes.

"You are still so young," said Keneben. "I had hoped Pharaoh would live long, so that you would be a grown man before you took his place."

"I am still young, as you say, and I may have only grown a little in height, but I have grown much in knowledge," Ramose said. "I have endured more than I thought possible, Keneben."

"You've had to look after yourself. Few princes know what it is like to be truly alone."

"I haven't been alone," Ramose said, glancing at Hapu and Karoya who were sitting further back in the boat. "I couldn't have done it without my friends."

"Your sister told me that you had loyal friends. But a prince should not have to suffer such hardship."

"It's made me stronger, Keneben. I believe I am ready to become the pharaoh, even if I am still young. If my father is ready to be united with the sun, I am ready to take my place on the throne of Egypt."

Ramose secretly hoped that the news that he was still alive would give his father a reason to hold on to life. He remembered the oracle's words. She had said he would see his father before he died. He didn't really believe that the old woman at the oasis could see people's futures, but her words encouraged him.

Ramose spent the time on the boat telling Keneben about his adventures. In his turn, Keneben recounted to Ramose all that had happened to him in Punt. Hapu and Karoya sat apart from them. In the evening, the boat was tied up and they sat on the banks of the river eating their evening meal. Ramose went over to his friends.

"I haven't seen much of you two," he said.

"You've been busy talking to your tutor," said Hapu.

"That doesn't mean that you can't sit with us."

"When you are the pharaoh," said Karoya, "you will not have time to sit and talk to slaves and apprentice painters."

"You'll be busy meeting with advisers, generals and foreign ambassadors," agreed Hapu.

Ramose had been concentrating so hard on how he would achieve his goal, he hadn't given much thought to what he would actually do when he became the pharaoh.

"I'll talk to whomever I please when I'm the pharaoh," he said grandly. "I'll free all slaves. I'll increase the wage of apprentice painters. I'll give every Egyptian free cakes on my birthday!"

"You'll be a popular pharaoh," laughed Karoya.

For the first time, Ramose allowed himself to believe that he really was going home. He chatted all evening, about going back to the palace, about sleeping in his own bed, about the jewellery he would have made for his sister.

"You'll have to discuss with the vizier how you want to rule Egypt," said Hapu.

Mention of the vizier spoiled Ramose's good mood. He hadn't considered how he would deal with his enemy when he became the pharaoh.

"I will appoint a new vizier," he said. "Someone I can rely on. Someone I can trust."

The three friends ate in silence. No matter what Ramose said, they all knew that things would be different between them once they arrived in Thebes.

Two days later there was a glint of white and gold in the distance and Thebes lay before them. Ramose's heart started to race. He would soon be home. The green fields on either side of the river stopped at the foot of whitewashed walls. A hundred or more gold-tipped flagpoles rose into the air with coloured pennants flapping in the breeze.

Among the temple buildings on the east bank Ramose could see the twin black granite obelisks that his father had raised in the temple of Amun. They were covered with carved hieroglyphs praising Amun, each symbol filled with gold paint. On the west bank was the palace and behind it the cliffs that hid the Great Place.

Gardens grew down to the edge of the river. It looked so beautiful that Ramose felt tears filling his eyes. The gardens contained the same crops as the fields they had passed, but they were carefully planned so that the squares of lettuces and onions made an attractive pattern. There were also flower gardens. The red of poppies, the blue of cornflowers, and the yellow and white of daisies added colour to the beautiful scene.

Ramose was relieved to see that the patch of lotus pads was still floating on the river in front of the palace garden. It was before noon and the flowers were reaching up to the sun with their blue petals spread wide. Children were wading in the shallows. There wasn't a crocodile in sight.

7

ASCENT TO THE SUN

THERE WAS a strange atmosphere in Thebes. The city was bustling with activity. It was an anxious time for Egyptians. Everyone hoped and prayed that their pharaoh would live, but if he didn't, all had to be ready for the smooth transition to a new pharaoh. Egypt without a pharaoh was unthinkable.

Crowds of people were coming and going—all

involved in preparations. Ramose wanted to walk around the streets of Thebes, but Keneben hurried them straight to the house of his mother. She worked in the small temple of Hapi, god of the Nile, on the west bank of the river.

"You must not go out of the temple grounds, Highness," Keneben said. "We cannot take any risks now that you are so close."

"But I want to see my sister."

"I have told Princess Hatshepsut that you are here."

"You've seen her? How is she? Doesn't she want to see me?"

"She is longing to see you, but she agrees that we should wait until the vizier is out of the palace."

At first, Ramose was happy to rest and walk among the temple buildings. It was a pleasure to stroll through the gardens that stretched right to the river's edge. He delighted in showing Karoya and Hapu the places by the river where he had played as a child. They could hardly believe that their friend was the spoilt, unpleasant boy who had enjoyed making servants' lives miserable. Ramose couldn't believe it either.

After three days, Ramose had walked every path in the temple grounds five times over.

"We have to work out a plan, Keneben," he said. "I will have to sneak into the palace without being seen. You will have to get a disguise for me."

"You must be patient, Highness," the tutor replied. "You must promise me you will wait until I am sure it is safe."

Ramose promised that he would be patient, but it was hard when he was so close to the palace. He was no longer used to doing nothing. He'd waited too long. With the whitewashed walls of his home visible from the temple gardens, the temptation was too great.

"I'm going for a walk in the gardens," Ramose told his friends.

Hapu was busy teaching Karoya how to play senet.

Ramose walked through the temple vegetable garden and fig tree grove. He wandered past the stables where the oxen were kept. He strolled near the muddy area where the goose herder led the geese down to the riverbank. Without thinking about it, not consciously anyway, he had walked to the high wall that marked the end of the temple grounds. Beyond the wall was the palace. He walked in the shadow of the wall. He wasn't walking aimlessly now. There was something he was looking for.

The wall stretched in a straight line for many cubits, then it turned suddenly at a right angle in front of him. In the corner, at the bottom of the

wall, Ramose found what he was searching for.
A hole had been cut at the bottom of the mud
brick wall to allow water to drain from the courtyard within. It wasn't a big hole. It had been
Ramose's secret way out of the palace when he
was younger. Now it was going to be his way in.
He looked around. There was no one in sight. He
got down on his hands and knees and examined
the hole. It wasn't big enough for him to fit
through; he'd grown too much.

He searched the garden beds until he found a
sharp stone. He started to hack at the mud brick
around the edges of the hole. It was still a little
damp from the last time water had washed
through the hole. In a few minutes the hole was
big enough for him to wriggle through.

Ramose scrambled to his feet on the other side.
He was in a small courtyard. It was a place where
female servants sat when they were spinning or
sewing. Some herbs were growing in pots around
the walls but otherwise it was empty. It was just
as well. No one had complained about him being
there when he was a child. They might have felt
differently now that he was older.

He entered the palace. There was a sense of
quiet urgency in the corridors. Servants and officials moved swiftly but silently, each one with
their own purpose. He felt self-conscious at first,
imagining that people would notice him. But in

his simple kilt and reed sandals he looked just like a servant. There were hundreds of servants in the palace. No one knew them all. He walked with the same silent purpose as everyone else. No one even glanced at him. Now that he was there, he didn't try to pretend to himself that he hadn't intended to get into the palace. He knew exactly what he was going to do. He'd known it all along really.

It was strange being back in the palace. The corridors were wide, the rooms huge. Everywhere was smooth and clean. The legs of stools were carved into elegant lion paws or gazelle feet. The backs of chairs were decorated with delicate patterns of inlaid jewels. Almost every wall, floor and ceiling was painted with bright pictures or patterns.

He entered a wide corridor. On either side there were rows of stone statues—enormous seated figures of the royal ancestors. His grandfather and his great grandfather were among them. They stared across at each other with blank unseeing eyes. Ramose barely came up to their knees.

Ramose was afraid that he would run into someone who knew him. He kept his head bowed and tried not to look anyone in the eye. Then he realised that there was no one he knew. Not a single servant or official looked familiar. It was like a dream. Everything was so familiar, yet it had changed somehow. He was a stranger in his own home.

He walked through the western hall. The floor was painted green, dotted with bright painted flowers. The huge papyrus-topped columns towered over him. They too were brightly painted, covered in paintings and hieroglyphs recounting the pharaoh's deeds. Here was a painting of the pharaoh throwing a spear. There was the pharaoh with his foot on the head of an enemy.

Ramose had walked through this hall every day when he had lived in the palace. He had hardly been aware of the paintings. Now he was dazzled by the brilliance of the colours. When he was a child, he had never thought about the size of the columns. Now, even though he'd grown half a cubit since he was there last, he felt dwarfed by the enormous pillars of stone.

He turned a corner, then another, and opened a door. He was in his own room. Except that it looked nothing like his room. Papyrus scrolls lay on a table. A young apprentice was busily copying cursive writing from a large stone flake onto a papyrus. He looked up and then ignored Ramose.

The room had been turned into a scribe's office. His soft bed had gone. So had the chests that held his clothes and playthings. The lion-footed chair wasn't there either. If it hadn't been for the paintings of the god Amun on one wall and his father hunting on the other, Ramose would have thought he was in the wrong room. He'd imagined he was coming home, but the palace didn't feel like home at all.

Ramose followed another corridor that led to the other side of the palace. This corridor was less familiar. There was a blanket of silence over that part of the palace. No one was hurrying. Ramose only passed one servant. At the end of the corridor there was a doorway guarded by two palace guards each holding a long, curved dagger. It was the door to his father's private quarters.

Ramose thought back. He couldn't remember the last time he'd seen his father. Many seasons had passed since he'd left the palace. Before that, in the innocent days when he didn't know his life was in danger, his father had been away on a campaign in Kush for many months. Before that?

He searched his memory for a time when he had been with his father. He had a picture in his mind of his father hunting hippopotamus by the riverbank. It was a clear picture. Then Ramose realised that all he was remembering was the painting of his father in his own room—or what used to be his room.

The last memory he had of being in his father's presence was when he had been summoned to these very rooms. His father had lectured him about throwing rotten figs at the kitchen servants.

His father had told him it was not the behaviour of a future pharaoh.

Ramose had vague memories of happy times playing with his brothers before they died. He could hear a tinkling laugh and smell a particular combination of perfume and herbs, which he knew belonged to his mother. He had no pictures of her in his memory, though. Now, soldiers with daggers guarded his father's chamber and he had to think of a way to get past them.

"Don't loiter in the corridor, boy," said a voice behind him.

Ramose bowed his head. He didn't have to look up to know who had spoken. It was a deep growling voice. He would have known Vizier Wersu's voice anywhere. The vizier had slipped into the corridor and crept up behind Ramose without him realising.

"Fetch me a goblet of wine," ordered the vizier as he swept noiselessly into the pharaoh's quarters.

Ramose bowed his head even lower as he turned and went towards the kitchens. He knew the way from his childhood. When he was small he'd liked to go there and watch the bread being made. The servants would make special cakes for him shaped like animals. As he'd gotten older, he'd stopped going there. Instead, he'd sent Heria to return dishes untouched when he'd demanded something bigger, better or entirely different.

He still remembered the way to the kitchens, though.

No one questioned him. He tried to stop his hands from shaking as he filled a jar with wine and returned to his father's quarters. He held the jar before him and the guards lowered their daggers and let him pass.

He entered the pharaoh's audience hall. It was smaller than the ceremonial western hall, but still impressive. The floor was painted blue to represent a pool covered with lotus pads and flowers. Fish and frogs swam in the water. Painted ducks paddled around the edges. It was beautiful. The columns in this room were more slender and made of wood. Their tops were carved in the shape of lotus buds. On the ceiling, a painting of a huge vulture with its wings spread wide scowled down at Ramose. Its wings must have been ten cubits across. Ramose walked through the hall and into the throne room where the pharaoh's throne sat on a raised platform. The empty throne glittered with gold and jewels. On the steps leading up to the platform were paintings of foreign captives on their knees, bound together with a rope around their necks. Each time the pharaoh walked up the steps he would tread on his enemies.

Ramose walked through the throne room into the pharaoh's sitting room. Gold goblets and bowls sat unused on a low table. There was a couch made of ebony with carved legs and arms. The rare wood was usually used only to make small items such as jewellery boxes. The wood in the couch was probably worth more than the gold and jewels that decorated it. Ramose thought back and could only remember a handful of times when he'd been in the room before. He picked up one of the goblets and filled it with wine.

Another doorway led to the pharaoh's bed-chamber. Ramose entered the room. Looking through his fringe he glanced over to the bed. Ramose could not see his father for the crowd of people standing around his bed. He thought for one dreadful moment that his father must have just died. He was wrong. It was a group of priests muttering prayers. Pharaoh's physician was there as well, mixing a foul-looking brown potion. The vizier was standing to one side.

Only one of the high windows was unshuttered, so the room was dim. With his head bowed low and his heart thudding, Ramose handed the goblet to the vizier. The vizier didn't even glance at him. Ramose backed away like a good servant, but when the vizier turned his attention back to the bed, Ramose sidestepped into the pharaoh's robing room.

It was unlikely that Pharaoh would ever be left alone, but Ramose had to hope. He sat in a corner and waited. Even that small, unlit room was lavishly painted. He sat down on a stool and rested his head against a wall painted with a grapevine pattern. The sound of the priests' chanting made him drowsy. The ceiling was covered with a spiral pattern. He was mesmerised by the swirling shapes. The chanting suddenly stopped and Ramose sat up with a start. Once again, his first thought was that the pharaoh had died. The priests and the doctor filed out. Vizier Wersu followed them. There was no wailing, no sounds of grief. Ramose was relieved to realise that it was only time for the midday meal.

One elderly priest was left to keep watch over the dying pharaoh. He was soon dozing. Ramose crept into the room so that he could see his father. Now he was so close he began to worry. Seeing his dead son appear at his bedside could easily make Pharaoh die of shock. He looked at the figure lying on the bed. What he saw was an old, old man. A man so thin and feeble it was impossible to imagine that he was the most powerful person in Egypt, that he was a god on Earth. The frail body looked nothing like the powerful, erect figure Ramose had just seen in the palace paintings, nothing like the memories he had of his father.

The priest's head dropped to his chest. Ramose crept to the bed. He thought that his father was sleeping, but when he leant closer, he saw that he was awake.

Ramose looked down at the old man's face. He opened his mouth but couldn't speak. Tears ran down his face and fell on the bed sheet. One tear fell on his father's hand. The hand rustled on the linen sheet like a dried vine leaf.

A pair of pale, watery eyes turned to him. The eyes looked at Ramose blankly.

"It's me. Ramose, your son. I didn't die. There was a...misunderstanding. I have travelled. I have learned much."

Ramose gently took the dried-up hand in his. "Father, I don't want to alarm you. I know you are ill, but I have to speak to you."

The eyes stared at him unblinking. His father had no idea who he was.

"Father, I am Ramose. I have come to take my place as your elder son...as your heir."

The dry, white lips moved, but no sound came out.

"Are you thirsty, Father?" asked Ramose.

He hurried out to the sitting room. The jar of wine he had brought from the kitchens was empty. He poured out a goblet of water instead.

"Here," he said. "There's no wine, but the waters of the Nile taste better than wine."

The old man raised his head a finger-width, but could get no further. Ramose helped him to sit up.

He held the goblet to his father's lips. A few drops of the water trickled into his mouth. His tongue ran along his lips moistening them with the river water. The old man's eyes found Ramose's again. He looked at him for a long time.

"Ramose," he whispered. The words came slowly as if each one was a great effort. "I have looked forward to meeting you and your brothers in the underworld."

"Yes, Father," said Ramose, his heart beating fast, tears running down his face. "It's me, Father. But I'm alive. I've been in hiding."

The old man smiled at his son. He raised his frail hand. Ramose felt the dry skin gently rasp his cheek. Then his eyes closed, his hand dropped to the bed. Ramose felt the body in his arms turn from a living thing to a lifeless shell as the spirit left. He laid his father down gently. His face still held the trace of a smile.

8

GHOST IN THE SCOOLROOM

SOMEONE HURRIED into the room. Ramose didn't move.

"Ramose," the person said. "I thought I would find you here."

It was Keneben.

"My father is mingling with the sun," said Ramose. "He's dead."

"May Amun protect him."

Keneben touched Ramose's shoulder. "You can't stay here, Highness. It is too dangerous."

Ramose looked up at his tutor. He wasn't sure how long he'd been sitting there in silence at the side of his dead father. It could have been a few seconds or an hour.

"I wanted to tell father about my adventures," said Ramose softly. "When I was young, he always thought I was foolish. I wanted him to be proud of me."

"Priest," said Keneben sharply. "Wake up, priest. Pharaoh has rested from life."

The priest woke with a jolt. He looked from the stern face of the tutor to the servant boy weeping silently over the lifeless form of the pharaoh.

"Don't just sit there, Priest!" said Keneben. "Get the physician."

The priest tripped on the hem of his robes as he stumbled out of the room.

"Come, Prince Ramose," said Keneben. "We must plan what to do next."

"I have to see my sister," said Ramose. "I have to tell her."

"Princess Hatshepsut is not in the palace." Keneben's voice softened when he spoke of the princess.

"Where is she?"

"She is at the women's palace."

"Why isn't she at father's side?"

"Queen Mutnofret found it too distressing to be near the pharaoh in his illness. She insisted that the princess went with her."

The women's palace was an hour's journey by boat south of Thebes. Ramose's sadness was replaced by anger at the mention of the hated queen's name.

"I have to go to Hatshepsut," he said, rushing to the door.

"Wait, Highness," said Keneben, holding out a hand to stop him. "I will send a message to her. She will return immediately."

"But the new pharaoh must be proclaimed tomorrow at dawn. I have to reveal myself."

"It is a long time till dawn. We have to keep you safe till then."

Ramose hesitated at the door.

"Wait until Princess Hatshepsut returns. With her support you will be safe."

Ramose sighed.

"You must go back to my mother's house, Highness," said Keneben. "Your friends are concerned about you."

The thought of seeing his friends again warmed Ramose's chilled heart. He turned to his father's body.

"I don't want to leave Father alone though. Will you stay with him until the priests return?"

Keneben seemed reluctant to let his young

master out of his sight, but eventually agreed to meet Ramose back at his mother's house.

Ramose walked cautiously through the corridors of the palace. He didn't want to run into the priests or the vizier. The palace was massive, bigger than many of the towns he had passed through on his travels. He chose a different route to reach the servants' quarters.

First, he went through a side door in the pharaoh's audience hall that led to a private courtyard. Then he walked down the narrow path that the gardeners used to reach the courtyard because they were not permitted to walk through the pharaoh's quarters.

He climbed over a low wall into an open area where the pharaoh's horses were kept. Beyond the stables was the wing of the palace that used to be known as the princes' palace. That was where his own room was and where his older brothers quarters had been before they died. It was also where the schoolroom was. As Ramose passed the familiar door, he couldn't resist peering in.

The schoolroom hadn't changed at all. There were no bright wall paintings there, just plain, whitewashed walls. On one wall, some hieroglyphs had been hastily drawn in charcoal. Ramose recognised Keneben's handwriting. He often used the walls to demonstrate the correct way to draw a particular hieroglyph. A papyrus was pinned to another wall. Ramose looked closer. It was the one about the benefits of being a scribe, Keneben's favourite text. There were reed mats on the floor for students to sit on. The only furniture was the graceful chair where Hatshepsut sat. He was pleased to think that his sister had kept up her studies. He was sure that she would be a valuable adviser to him when he became pharaoh.

Ramose was suddenly aware that he wasn't the only one in the room. He spun round. A young boy was standing in the doorway with an elegant ebony palette and pen box under his arm. When the boy saw Ramose's face, he dropped the palette and it shattered on the floor.

"Ramose?" said the boy in a faltering voice. "Is that you, Ramose?"

It was Tuthmosis, Ramose's half-brother, the snivelling son of Queen Mutnofret.

"Are you a ghost?" he said in a frightened voice.

"No," replied Ramose coldly. "I'm real."

The boy rushed towards Ramose who stood ready to defend himself. But the boy didn't attack him, instead he flung his arms around his neck.

"You're still alive!" Tuthmosis said. "I can't believe it."

"That's right." Ramose pulled the boy away. He was surprised to see a smile on his face. "That's the end of your scheme."

"What scheme?" The boy's brow creased.

"Well, I suppose it's your mother's scheme."

Tuthmosis looked genuinely puzzled.

"I've come to take my rightful place as the pharaoh," Ramose said.

The boy smiled again. "That's wonderful."

"Don't play act with me," said Ramose angrily.

"Where have you been these past seasons?" continued Tuthmosis. "Mother told me you'd died. Wait till she hears—"

"I know all about the plan to kill me."

"Who tried to kill you?" asked the prince, grabbing hold of Ramose's arm.

"You know very well who. Your mother."

"Don't be silly, Ramose. Why would she do that?"

"So that you could be the pharaoh."

The boy laughed. "But I don't have to be the pharaoh now. You're here."

"Don't you want to be the pharaoh?"

"No! Ever since you…died…I haven't been allowed outside the palace. I'm not permitted to play with the other palace children and I can't visit the servants' quarters any more. I have to spend more time here studying, so that I can be a great pharaoh like father. I hate it."

Ramose didn't know what to say. He thought the boy must be lying, but he didn't think he was clever enough to put on such a convincing display.

He heard footsteps in the hall. "We need to go somewhere where we can talk without being disturbed."

"I know a place," said Tuthmosis.

Ramose could scarcely believe he was allowing the young prince to lead him by the hand, but he did. Tuthmosis led him to a narrow staircase that went up to the roof. He zigzagged across the roofs until he came to the western hall, which rose up higher than the other buildings. More steps led to a ledge where a shuttered window let light into the vast hall below. There was a stool in a corner that couldn't be seen from anywhere in the palace.

"I come here when I want to get away from everyone," said the young prince.

Ramose couldn't believe it. He had used the same hiding place when he was younger.

Ramose sat down on the dusty stool and looked at the boy. He had grown taller since he'd seen him last. He had lost all his puppy fat. The mischievous glint in his eyes had been replaced with a worried, almost frightened look. His fingernails were bitten down.

"What has happened to you over the past year, Brother?" the boy asked eagerly. "Tell me everything."

Ramose told him all about the attempt to kill him, his escape to the Great Place, his journey towards Memphis to see Pharaoh, his adventures at the pyramid and in the desert. Tuthmosis sat with his mouth open, listening to everything with amazement.

"But who would want you dead?" asked the boy with tears in his eyes.

"I believe it was your mother and the vizier who planned to murder me," said Ramose.

Tears flew in all directions as Tuthmosis shook his head vigorously.

"No, that can't be. Mother wouldn't do such a terrible thing."

"I think she would do anything to make you pharaoh, and with the vizier encouraging her…"

"But I don't want to be the pharaoh."

"There is something else, Pegget," said Ramose.

Tuthmosis smiled and wiped away his tears. "You haven't called me that since I was a small child."

The word meant frog. "It isn't a very nice name, I suppose," said Ramose, feeling guilty.

"I like it," said Tuthmosis. "It's the sort of name an older brother should use for his younger brother."

Ramose felt even guiltier. He had never thought of Tuthmosis as a brother. Not like his older brothers. And yet they had the same father. He could see they both had the same large ears, long fingers and a way of turning their mouths down instead of up when they smiled—just like their father.

"What else do you have to tell me?" Tuthmosis asked. "I hope it's not as upsetting as the rest."

"It is worse, Pegget," Ramose replied. "It's Father, he has ascended to the sun. He died at midday. I was with him."

Tears flowed again from the boy's eyes. Ramose put his arm around his brother's shoulder.

"You've come just in time then," said the boy wiping his eyes on his kilt. "You can take your place as Pharaoh's elder son and heir."

"I have to wait until our sister returns to the palace. I need her support."

Tuthmosis nodded, though he looked a little timid at the mention of Hatshepsut.

"Your mother won't be so pleased to see me, though," said Ramose.

"It doesn't matter. You're here. You are the true heir. There's nothing she can do to change that."

Ramose wasn't so sure.

"I'll stay in hiding until just before dawn," said Ramose.

Tuthmosis hugged his brother. "I'll do whatever I can to help you. May the gods protect you."

Ramose turned and left. He didn't know what to think. He wanted to believe that Tuthmosis was telling the truth, that the boy didn't know about the poisoning, that he didn't mind if he wasn't the pharaoh. Ramose stumbled down the steps in confusion—and into the arms of two palace guards.

The guards each grabbed hold of one of Ramose's arms.

"Let me go," he yelled. "Do you know who I am?"

One of the guards chuckled to himself. The other took a wooden club from his belt and Ramose watched as it curved towards him and crashed into his head.

9

THE BEE IN THE LOTUS

RAMOSE AWOKE to find himself in a dark room with his arms and legs tied up. The walls were roughly plastered with mud. Faint light seeped in through the cracks in the door. The earth floor was covered with straw that smelt of pig urine. It wasn't a room, it was a pigsty.

He wriggled his hands and feet to try and free

himself from the ropes, but all that did was make his wrists and ankles sore. He thought back to his meeting with Prince Tuthmosis. The boy had tricked him with his hugs and his tears. It must have all been a sham. Without Ramose noticing, the boy had somehow alerted the guards to come and capture him. He felt foolish that he had fallen for such a ploy.

Struggling to his knees, Ramose shuffled around his prison. He searched every finger-width of the foul place in search of something that could cut through the ropes. There was nothing. He strained against his bonds until his wrists were bleeding, furious that he'd been bound and imprisoned like a foreign captive, like a pig ready for slaughter. In anger and frustration, he threw himself against the door again and again until he fell back to the stinking floor, exhausted.

He had to think. Anger would achieve nothing. He only had a few hours until the succession ceremony that would proclaim the next pharaoh. He had to get out of his prison. He couldn't think of anything he could do. The light seeping in through the cracks faded.

The sound of a bolt sliding startled him. A servant entered holding a lamp. The light reflected in his frightened eyes. Another servant followed carrying a bowl and a cup. He put them down in the straw. Neither said a word, but outside Ramose could hear a voice—a stern female voice.

"He must stay there until after dawn." The voice sent a cold shiver down his spine. It was sweet sounding, but cruel at the same time. "If he escapes, you won't see another morning."

Ramose knew the voice. He knew it well. As the servants hurried out, Ramose could see briefly through the doorway. There was a blur of bright white in the lamplight, a flash of gold, a glint of turquoise. There was a waft of perfume. Ramose tried to cry out but his voice caught in his throat. It was Hatshepsut, his sister. She was the one who had imprisoned him.

Ramose sat in the dark and tried to make sense of it. Perhaps he was mistaken. Perhaps he'd misheard what she'd said. Perhaps it wasn't her he'd seen at all. It had just been a glimpse, a few seconds in dim light. He argued back and forth with himself for some time, but in his heart he had no doubt. His sister had betrayed him.

Through all the time that he had been away, Ramose had endured the hardship and disappointment with the thought that his sister was waiting for him, missing him, praying for his safety. It had helped to keep him going. But all that time she had kept a terrible secret. She didn't want Ramose to be the pharaoh at all. Instead it was the half-brother who they had both despised that she wanted to rule Egypt. Why? Did she hate him so much? Did she think Tuthmosis would make a better pharaoh?

Everything Ramose believed had been turned upside down. He slumped to the floor, his face in the foul straw, and wept. He cried out in pain and misery. He was alone in the world, completely alone. His loved ones had slowly been stripped away from him one by one. First, his mother, whom he could hardly remember. Then his older brothers, then Heria, his beloved nanny, and, only hours ago, his father. Now he had discovered that his only remaining family, his sister whom he had trusted completely, had turned against him.

Ramose thought of Keneben; perhaps he would come and free him. His tutor had risked everything for him before. Surely he wouldn't let him down now. But would the gentle tutor be able to stand up to the vizier and Hatshepsut? Ramose had felt lonely on his travels, but he'd always had the thought of coming home. Now he was home and he was more alone than he'd ever been. He sobbed out loud, not caring who heard him. He sobbed until every scrap of his energy was gone.

Ramose lay with his face squashed into the dirty straw for hours. His mind was blank. Every thought was painful. It was better not to think at all. His left arm was numb beneath him. His foot was prickling as if someone were sticking sewing needles into it.

He heard movement in the straw behind him, a faint rustle. He thought for a moment that there must have been another prisoner whom he hadn't noticed in the darkness. Then he saw a little creature run across the floor to the bowl of food. He could see it by the faint light from the guard's lamp that seeped in through the cracks in the door. It was a mouse. The little creature sat no more than half a cubit from Ramose's head, nibbling on a piece of bread. It was such a delicate creature, so small. Every day it had to risk its life just to feed itself. It had to creep out at night to steal food, living in constant fear of the palace cats that wanted nothing more than to crunch its fragile bones. He didn't disturb the mouse. He let it eat its fill.

Ramose suddenly remembered Karoya and Hapu. He'd been so busy feeling sorry for himself, he hadn't given a thought to them. What would Hatshepsut do with his friends? The two people in all of Egypt that he knew he could rely on, the ones who had voluntarily stayed with him through all sorts of danger and hardship. He felt ashamed that he had forgotten them.

He scrambled painfully to his knees and wriggled his fingers until the feeling came back into them. The mouse sat watching him. The mouse hadn't died, so he knew the food wasn't poisoned. He needed to eat. He had a lot to do. With difficulty he picked up the cup of water with his bound hands and drank. He picked up the remains of the bread, now dried up and mouse-nibbled. He scraped up the cold lentil stew with the bread and ate it all. It wasn't the best meal he'd ever had, but it wasn't the worst either. He sat up and felt his strength and determination return. He'd been in worse situations. He'd been lost in the desert, buried alive in a tomb, washed away by a flood. He'd survived all of that. Escaping from a pigsty shouldn't be difficult.

He picked up the empty bowl and struggled to his feet. He shuffled back and forth until he had cleared away the straw from an area of the earth floor. He raised the bowl as high above his head as he could and then with all his strength he flung it onto the cleared patch of floor. The bowl shattered. Ramose knelt down and examined the pieces. A hint of a smile crept over his face as he picked up one long shard with a sharp edge.

He sat with his back against the wall. He gripped the shard firmly between his feet and began to rub the cords that bound his hands backwards and forwards across the shard. The rope was made of twisted reeds. He cut through it fibre by fibre. It was slow work, but Ramose had no doubt that he could do it. Once his hands were free, he started to cut through the rope around his feet. The whole process must have taken two hours, but Ramose kept at it without stopping. Finally, the ropes around his ankles fell away. He walked around the cell for a few minutes until his legs lost their stiffness.

The room was built to imprison pigs, not people. The roof was low and made of two wooden beams with palm branches laid across them which were plastered over with a thin layer of mud. Ramose jumped up and grabbed at one of the palm branches. It was brittle from years of baking in the sun. It broke in half. He pulled the branch down and then another. The thin mud plaster crumbled and showered down on him. Ramose smiled to himself as he looked up at the black sky pricked with the light of the number-less stars. He jumped up again and grasped hold of one of the solid wooden beams with both hands. Then he swung up his leg. He hooked his foot around the beam at the second go and gradually managed to hoist himself up.

He inched his way along the beam. A thin sliver of moon was reclining low in the sky. It gave next to no light but there was enough light from blaz-ing torches dotted around the palace walls for him to get his bearings. The preparations for the dawn ceremony were underway. Ramose guessed it was less than two hours before dawn. There wasn't much time until the ceremony began, but first, Ramose had something to do. He had to find out if his friends were safe.

He jumped down from the pigsty roof. But instead of heading towards the western hall, he turned the other way and retraced his steps towards the temple. He found the servants' quarters, slipped through the hole in the wall and ran through the darkened gardens towards Keneben's mother's house.

The house was in darkness. Ramose crept in. He tiptoed to the room where he and Hapu had slept. Hapu wasn't there. He went up the garden steps to the roof. Karoya wasn't there either. Their bags were gone. There was no sign that they had ever been there. He went back down the steps and into the house. Keneben's bed was empty and hadn't been slept in. Ramose had a bad feeling. If his sister had turned against him, his friends weren't safe.

By the time he had run back to the palace the area around the western hall was buzzing with activity. Ramose was puzzled. The succession was a simple ceremony only involving the new pharaoh and the head priest. It had to take place at dawn the day after the old pharaoh's death. Egypt without a pharaoh was a terrible thing. Without a pharaoh to take charge of the country, without the god-king ruling the land, Egypt would dissolve into chaos. Dreadful things would happen: disease, famine, defeat at the hands of enemies. It was vital that the new pharaoh be in place as soon as possible. The coronation itself would be a lavish ceremony with rituals, a sacrifice to the gods and a banquet lasting for days. That would wait until after the old pharaoh's funeral.

Ramose's heart was thudding, partly because he was running hard, partly because in the next hour or so he would become Pharaoh of Egypt. He would be king; he would have a place among the gods. But he didn't feel any different to any other day. There was no spark within him that might grow into a divine flame.

When he was a spoilt prince who only knew the inside of one palace or another, he had never doubted that he'd make a good pharaoh. Now, after living among ordinary Egyptians, after walking the length of Egypt, he felt decidedly unroyal, certainly not god-like. He knew more about his country and its people than he ever had before, but he'd learned how to be ordinary. What if he wasn't a good pharaoh? What if he let his people down?

He decided the best place to wait for the ceremony to start was up on the roof. He climbed up the stairs to Tuthmosis's private place. He peered through the window, cautiously. Far below in the glow of dozens of lamps, people hurried back and forth. Workmen were erecting a raised platform for the throne at one end of the hall. Chairs for officials were being arranged around the platform. Shrines and statues were being carried in. Ramose decided to wait until the perfect moment when he could walk into the hall and declare that it was his right to take his place as the next pharaoh. He pulled the stool over to where he could sit comfortably and have a good view through the window.

He woke with a start when the priests below started chanting. He had meant to stay awake, but somehow he had dozed off. The sky was a warm rosy colour. Ramose realised that the ceremony had already started. He rubbed his eyes and peered in through the window.

The hall was full of people. The government officials, leaders of the army, and two chiefs from foreign lands sat on one side. On the other side were priests, many priests. Walking down the aisle, Vizier Wersu led palace officials carrying the standards of the royal ancestors on tall poles. A high priest, with his leopard skin draped over one shoulder, followed behind. The air was thick with incense.

Behind the high priest came Prince Tuthmosis. He was being carried on a chair, not by servants, but on the shoulders of eight government ministers. Servants on either side of him waved ostrich feather fans.

Following the prince were Queen Mutnofret and Princess Hatshepsut. Both were dressed in royal splendour. They wore long dresses. The Queen's had a pattern of snakes' heads embroidered on the hem. Hatshepsut's had a beaded sash. Their jewellery—heavy beaded collars on their shoulders and bracelets on their wrists and upper arms—glittered in the lamplight.

The queen wore a wig on top of which was a golden crown. Hatshepsut's hair had been braided into hundreds of tiny plaits. Each plait was decorated with rings of gold placed at intervals down its length. She wore a type of crown that Ramose had never seen before. As well as the raised snake's head, there was also a golden vulture's head rearing from her forehead. The wings of the vulture, made of hundreds of tiny pieces of jasper and lapis lazuli, draped down on either side of her head. She carried a blue lotus flower.

His sister's face had lost all of its girlish prettiness. It was still a most beautiful face, but it was also frightening. The dark vulture's wings gave her a threatening look. Her black-ringed eyes had a strange, hard gloss. He didn't understand what had happened to his sister. She had loved him, he was sure. What had made her become so cold and hard? Why had she turned against him? Ramose's eyes filled with tears again as he grieved for his sister's lost love. He wiped his eyes, then stood up and straightened his kilt. It was time.

All eyes were fixed on the glittering procession which had now reached the foot of the throne. The officials took their places. No one noticed Ramose enter the hall—no one except Vizier Wersu. The vizier's crocodile eyes were looking right into Ramose's. He had seen him and he knew who he was. Ramose saw the vizier turn to his men. He felt his courage fail him. It was only for a moment though. No matter what happened he knew he couldn't turn back now.

The ministers lowered the chair and Tuthmosis stepped down. He knelt before the dual shrines of Upper and Lower Egypt, barefoot and wearing nothing but a simple white kilt. Even from the back of the hall, Ramose could see the young prince shaking with fear and nervousness. The splendid decorations, the standards, the many priests, all dwarfed the small figure. He looked nothing like a pharaoh, nothing like a god. He looked exactly like a frightened little boy.

Two priests, one wearing the falcon mask of Horus, the other wearing the mask of the strange Seth creature, took a crown from each of the shrines—the white crown of Upper Egypt and the red crown of Lower Egypt. Other priests carried the royal crook and flail, symbols of kingship.

Ramose realised with a shock that this ceremony was more than a simple succession to prevent the chaos of Egypt without a pharaoh. This was also the full coronation rushed forward before the old pharaoh was even buried. This had never happened before. If his guess was right, Queen Mutnofret and the vizier were trying to prevent Ramose from having any chance of claiming the throne.

Ramose realised that Wersu was no longer on the stage. He glanced around but couldn't see him. The high priest stepped forward and spoke.

"Our Pharaoh has ascended to heaven. He is united with the sun." The priest's voice echoed around the hall. "Now the sun disc has risen from the land of light, the gods must choose a new pharaoh."

Ramose was just about to shout out and make his presence known when two things happened. First he saw two faces in the crowd that had been hidden from his view up on the roof. A chill crept over him. The faces belonged to Keneben and Hapu. Keneben was staring adoringly, not at the future pharaoh, but at the figure of Princess Hatshepsut who was sinking gracefully onto an elegant throne-like chair at the side of the platform. Her women arranged the folds of her gown.

She slowly raised the blue lotus flower to her nose to inhale its fragrance. Hapu was looking at her as well—not in admiration, but in fear. The words of the oracle came back to Ramose: the blue lotus can hide a bee in its petals. His sister had turned Keneben against him. After his years of loyalty to Ramose, he now supported Tuthmosis. Poor Hapu was powerless against her. Perhaps he too would fall under her spell. The sting of this bee was far worse than the scorpion sting.

The second thing that happened was a faint, hoarse voice behind him calling out his name. Ramose turned. A line of criminals was being led past the hall. Their hands were bound behind them. They were linked together like animals by a rope around their necks, like the figures of the enemies of Egypt painted on steps for the pharaoh to tread on.

There were two Egyptians, each with a hand or an ear cut off, indicating that they had already committed other crimes. There were three Libyans. Ramose recognised them by their beards, their long hair and the bands of leather that crossed their chests. Behind them were four people from Kush, easily recognisable by their black skin. The last one in the line was Karoya. She was staring pleadingly at Ramose. They barely had time to exchange a glance before the other prisoners yanked her along. Stumbling to her knees and struggling to regain her footing, she was dragged off around a corner.

Ramose heard his half-brother speaking in a quavering voice.

"Hear me, mighty Ra. I stand before you, ready to take my father's place."

Ramose looked back at the empty passage where Karoya had just stood, dirty and dishevelled, with her dress torn and a look of terror in her eyes. He had a decision to make—a decision that would affect the rest of his life.

More of the oracle's words came back to him. "A perfect jewel will remain buried in the earth, yet the maid at the millstone holds it out in her hand." Suddenly, he knew what the oracle had meant. Friendship was more precious than any jewel, more important even than becoming the pharaoh. He ran out of the hall after Karoya. She was a true friend. He had to help her.

Ramose had seen criminals and foreign captives taken away before. They were put in boats and taken somewhere to the south. He didn't know where. Whether they were imprisoned, enslaved or executed, he had no idea. Such things hadn't interested him before. He had to get to the palace wharf quickly. He knew every palm-width of the palace better than any servant did because he had access to all the royal apartments. He knew the palace better than any official because as a child he'd wandered through the servants' quarters and the kitchens. There was no one who knew the palace better than Ramose.

He ran through back corridors to the kitchens where he stole a sharp cutting stone. He crossed forgotten courtyards, scurried across roofs and reached the palace wharf before the guards and their prisoners. A boat was being prepared for sailing. Ramose managed to slip aboard while the boatman was attending to the sail. He hid at the stern beneath one of the rowers' benches.

It wasn't long before the guards arrived with their prisoners, swearing at them and pushing them to make them hurry. They seemed to take particular pleasure in pushing and prodding Karoya. Ramose wanted to jump out and attack the guards, but he knew that wouldn't help. He had to work out a way to get Karoya free, but not end up tied to the chain of prisoners himself.

The captives were pushed on board and the guards undid the cords binding their wrists. The prisoners were to row themselves to whatever punishment awaited them. One guard stayed on board. The other returned to the riverbank and gave the order to cast off. The boatman untied the boat and took his position at the rudder. The guard gave another order and the prisoners began to row. Karoya was sitting on the last bench. Ramose touched her foot. She jumped up with a squeal.

"Sit down, slave girl," shouted the boatman. "You'll do your share of the rowing or I'll toss you over the side."

Karoya looked at Ramose with eyes like a rabbit about to have its neck broken. He gave her what he hoped was an encouraging signal, though he didn't really have any idea what he was going to do.

Once they had drawn clear of Thebes, the guard sat down and pulled some bread and figs from a bag at his feet. Ramose leapt out. The boatman cried out in surprise and let go of the rudder. Ramose gave him a hefty push and the boatman pitched into the river.

The guard, with his mouth full of bread and a fig in each hand, moved clumsily to unsheathe his dagger. Ramose was quicker. He grasped the handle of the dagger and pulled it out. The guard made a grab for him and Ramose swung the dagger, cutting deep into the guard's fleshy arm. As the guard cried out and grabbed his arm, Ramose elbowed him in the stomach as hard as he could. The guard tumbled into the fast-flowing waters with an enormous splash.

The prisoners were all staring in astonishment, their oars hanging motionless. The boatman was trying to clamber back over the side. The guard surfaced, spluttering and swearing, and started to splash back towards the boat.

"Row!" shouted Ramose, stamping on the boatman's fingers so that he let go and fell back into the river. "Row!"

The startled prisoners rowed for all they were worth. When they were clear of the struggling guard and boatman, Ramose made them row to the shore. He cut Karoya free and handed the blade to the nearest captive. He and Karoya jumped ashore and the prisoners rowed off. Ramose hoped they found freedom.

"We have to get back to the palace," Ramose told Karoya. "The coronation is taking place."

Karoya didn't understand what he meant.

"Pharaoh has died. They're crowning my half-brother this morning—now."

Ramose turned to run back to the palace and found himself face to face with the vizier.

10

FRIENDS AND ENEMIES

VIZIER WERSU had his ceremonial sceptre in his hand. He raised it above his head ready to use it as a weapon. Ramose remembered the vision in the desert—the vizier hitting him with the Seth statue. Behind him Karoya screamed. The guard that they had pushed overboard had crawled ashore and grabbed her by the ankle. The vizier suddenly rushed forward. He moved fast, like a crocodile striking. The sceptre fell, a bronze blur. Ramose flinched, expecting the sceptre to crash down on his head, but to his surprise, it didn't. It fell on the guard, knocking him back into the river.

"Come quickly," the vizier said. "You don't have much time. The new pharaoh is about to be proclaimed."

Ramose didn't move. He stared at the crocodile-faced vizier. Why was his enemy helping him?

"Come, Highness." Ramose felt the vizier's insect fingers clutch at his arm. Ramose hesitated, unable to believe that the man he had feared all his life was now on his side. Then he remembered the oracle's words—trust the crocodile. Karoya pushed him from behind.

"Hurry, Ramose."

Ramose ran, spurred on by the vizier in front and Karoya behind. Three palace guards marched towards them at one stage, but the vizier ordered them to search the river for the missing slaves. Ramose's head was spinning. There had to be another explanation for this. It had to be a trap. It wasn't possible that the vizier was helping him.

They reached the hall. Tuthmosis was seated on the throne. He now had a deep collar made of gold and turquoise resting on his shoulders. His arms were crossed over his chest. In one hand he held the royal crook, in the other the flail. The falcon-headed priest placed the white crown on his head. The Seth-beast priest placed the red crown on top of it. Together they formed the double crown of all Egypt. Ramose opened his mouth to shout out an objection. At that moment a ray of sunlight shot down from one of the high windows. The light illuminated the dust and incense smoke in its path, turning them into beautiful golden specks and swirls. The golden ray fell on Tuthmosis's head.

"Hail Tuthmosis," said the high priest. "King of Upper Egypt, King of Lower Egypt, Chosen of Ra, Beloved of Amun, strong in truth, protector of Egypt, subduer of her enemies."

Everyone in the hall responded. "Hail Tuthmosis."

Ramose walked up towards the platform. Like everyone else, his eyes were on Tuthmosis. The boy seemed to have grown in the short time Ramose had been out of the hall. The sunlight reflected on the gold of the crook and the flail and the snakehead on the double crown. It turned Tuthmosis's skin to gold as well. He no longer looked frightened.

Ramose realised he was too late. The gods had selected their pharaoh. It was stupid of him to think that he could have influenced the will of the gods. He kept walking until he was at the foot of the platform. Priests started forward to grab him. Tuthmosis stood up.

"Leave him alone," he said. Even his voice was stronger.

The priests obeyed their pharaoh and let Ramose approach the platform. Tuthmosis held out the crook to Ramose, offering it to him. Ramose walked up the two steps.

"Hail Tuthmosis," he said so that everyone could hear him. "Pharaoh of all Egypt."

He knelt at his brother's feet. The oracle's final words echoed in his mind—bow down before the frog.

"You are Pharaoh, Pegget," Ramose said in a quieter voice so that only his brother could hear him. "It is the will of the gods. I am here to serve you."

"Are you sure, Ramose?" asked Tuthmosis. "Is this what you want?"

Ramose nodded.

"But what will become of you? What will you do?"

"Might I suggest, Highness, that Prince Ramose be proclaimed as your adviser?"

Ramose and Tuthmosis turned. It was the vizier, who had slipped back into his position on the platform. There was a murmur of surprise in the hall as people realised who Ramose was.

Both boys nodded.

"Swear him in immediately, Vizier Wersu," said Tuthmosis.

The high priest opened his mouth to object.

"High Priest," said Tuthmosis in his new commanding voice. "Say a prayer to bless my adviser."

The high priest bowed in obedience. The vizier muttered a few important sounding words. The high priest said a blessing. Tuthmosis raised Ramose to his feet.

"Hail Ramose, Fan-bearer on the Right of the Pharaoh," said the vizier.

The crowd responded. "Hail Ramose."

Not everyone joined in the response this time. Ramose could see his sister and Queen Mutnofret staring at him with tightly closed mouths.

Tuthmosis climbed back onto the chair and was carried out into the sunlight. Four geese were released symbolising that news of the new pharaoh was to be carried to the four quarters of heaven. The pharaoh himself was to be taken across the river and carried around the walls of the Temple of Amun, so that the people of Thebes could honour him. After that he would have to travel throughout the land so that all Egyptians would know that chaos and disaster had been averted. Egypt had a new pharaoh.

Ramose lay on the bed in a guestroom in the palace, trying to make sense of everything that had happened. After months of endless waiting, after weeks of wandering about Egypt at a snail's pace, his world had changed in a matter of hours. He stared up at the bulls' heads painted on the ceiling. His dream of becoming the pharaoh was over. His half-brother was now king of all Egypt. Keneben, the tutor who had risked his life for him before, now served his sister. He still hadn't spoken to Hatshepsut, and now he wasn't sure if he wanted to.

There was a knock at the door and Vizier Wersu entered. That was another thing he'd been trying to come to terms with. This man, who, since his childhood, Ramose had considered to be his worst enemy, had turned out to be a friend.

"I have been unable to arrange a meeting with your sister, Your Excellency," he said, bowing.

Ramose sat up. "Where is she?"

"She has left for the women's palace again. She won't return until your father's funeral."

"Sit down, Vizier. There are some questions I'd like to ask you."

The vizier gathered his robes over one arm and sat down on a stool.

"What is it you want to know, Highness?"

"How exactly did you discover that I was still alive?"

The vizier smiled his crocodile smile. "I have spies all over Egypt. A little gold can be very persuasive. I heard that Keneben had hidden someone in a temple and then I learned that he was secretly arranging a position for an apprentice scribe in the Great Place."

"Why didn't you come and get me back then?"

"I believed Keneben's plan was a sound one. You were far safer there than in the palace. I had tried to keep an eye on you, but I did not know that Queen Mutnofret would stoop to murder. If Keneben and your nanny had not taken the precautions they did, you would have been poisoned."

"What about when I left the Great Place?"

"I lost track of you, I am afraid. I had people searching the country, but they couldn't find you. It wasn't until I heard news of tomb robbers in Lahun that my spies tracked you down. And then you slipped through their fingers again. Your skills at staying hidden are very impressive."

Ramose laughed. "There was no skill involved. I was just blundering around the country getting into trouble at every turn."

"Praise Amun, you are safe now."

Ramose looked at the vizier. "Why did you go to so much trouble to help me?"

"I serve the royal family," said the vizier. "You were the future pharaoh. It was my job to tend to your welfare."

"Did you suspect Queen Mutnofret?"

"No, Highness. I underestimated her. I wasn't concerned for your life, just your happiness. When your mother died and then your brothers, I could see that these losses affected you more than your sister. I did what I could to make them easier to bear."

"I had no idea."

"I convinced Pharaoh to delay your military training. I stopped him from taking Keneben to Punt with him. I saw to it that Heria, your nanny, stayed in the palace long after her duties were finished."

"It's hard for me to believe you have been looking out for me all this time. I thought you were my enemy."

"It was necessary to be stern. I knew you had a difficult path ahead of you." The vizier shook his head. "I didn't know just how difficult." Wersu stood up with a sigh. He looked old and tired.

"I'm sorry I didn't recognise your concern, Vizier. I was a selfish boy then."

"In the end I failed you. You were exposed to great danger. You did not take your rightful place on the throne."

"It is the will of the gods, Vizier."

"Aren't you disappointed, Ramose?" asked Karoya, as she walked down to the palace wharf with Ramose two days later.

"No," replied Ramose. "This is what was meant to be."

"But all the time I've known you, you've been working towards taking your place as the pharaoh. It's what you lived for." She stopped and looked at Ramose. "If you hadn't rescued me, you would be the pharaoh now."

Ramose shook his head. "The gods decide who will be the pharaoh, not lesser queens, not even royal princes."

"And you're not unhappy?"

"No," said Ramose, smiling at Karoya. She was wearing a beautiful gown and shawl made of blue cloth. It wasn't in the style of Egyptian clothing. It had been especially made for her in the style of the people of Kush.

"The only thing I regret is that my sister has become a stranger to me."

"I don't understand what happened to her. When I met her, back at the tomb makers' village, she seemed kind. And she seemed to love you."

"She became greedy for power."

"But she can never be the pharaoh."

"No, but she sees Tuthmosis as being a weak boy she can control."

Karoya shook her head. "I don't understand these things."

"Neither do I. That's why I'm leaving Thebes. I don't want to spend my life among such people."

"The oracle was wrong." said Karoya. "She told us that you would be the pharaoh."

"No. She said I would achieve my goal. My goal was to see my father before he died. I achieved that. I also wanted happiness. I would never have been happy as the pharaoh, constantly at war with my sister, afraid for my life."

"But you suffered so much."

"And I learnt a lot, Karoya—about Egypt and about myself. I've realised that I'm an odd sort of Egyptian. I have a liking for travel and a desire to get to know barbarians. I would never have found that out about myself if I had stayed in the palace."

"But being a fan-bearer sounds very dull," said Karoya.

Ramose laughed. "I don't actually have to sit at Pharaoh's side waving a fan, Karoya. Fan-bearer on the Right of the Pharaoh is a title. It's one of the highest positions in Egypt, next to the vizier. And Tuthmosis is happy to let me wander around Egypt and report on the situation at its borders. So he's given me another title—Superintendent of Foreign Lands."

"I'm glad you're coming with me," said Karoya.

"My first duty will be to deliver you back safely to your people."

Vizier Wersu was waiting for them at the wharf. He smiled as they approached. Ramose still thought he looked like a crocodile, but he had learned to like the vizier.

"I have carried out your wishes," the vizier told him. "Keneben will not be banished, but he is no longer the royal tutor. He will be posted in a lesser temple."

"And Queen Mutnofret?"

"She will be confined in a remote palace," the vizier replied. "It is more than she deserves."

Ramose nodded. He hadn't been able to bring himself to demand the death sentence she deserved. She was after all Tuthmosis's mother.

"There is someone who wishes to speak to you, Your Excellency," the vizier said.

A small figure with his head hung low came from behind the vizier. It was Hapu. The boy fell to his knees.

"I'm sorry, Your Excellency," he said, with tears streaming down his face. "I let you down. I could not do anything to stop the coronation."

"Get up, Hapu," said Ramose. "And for Amun's sake call me Ramose. There was nothing you could have done."

"I could have tried at least. I was afraid of Princess Hatshepsut," said Hapu, miserably.

"You were wise to fear her, Hapu. She is dangerous."

"Why don't you come to Kush with Ramose and me?" asked Karoya.

Hapu shook his head. "I don't want any more adventures. I just wish I could go back to the Great Place and be an apprentice painter again."

"I think that can be arranged." Ramose glanced at the vizier. The vizier nodded. "It will be good to have you working on my father's tomb. You can make sure the tomb makers do the job properly."

"Thank you, Ramose."

Ramose hugged his friend and then stepped aboard the boat. Karoya followed. The vizier, who was going with them as far as the first cataract, helped her aboard.

The boat pulled away from the wharf. Ramose waved goodbye to Hapu. Earlier, he had taken leave of his brother who had hugged him and told him he would miss him. He hadn't spoken to Hatshepsut. He had glimpsed her in a corridor, but she had turned away from him.

"Was my sister involved in the plot to poison me?" Ramose asked the vizier.

"No, Your Excellency, but in the months that you were absent, she developed a greed for power. She thought that she would make a better pharaoh than you or your brother. She planned to rule from behind the scenes. Not even Queen Mutnofret realised."

Ramose sighed. His sister was lost to him, but he had a brother now. He glanced at the vizier. And he had friends in very high places.

Karoya sat down next to him. Her face showed a mixture of joy because she was going home, and terror because she had to spend weeks on a boat with the Nile in flood. The boat plunged through the surging waters. Karoya held on to Ramose's arm.

The wind filled the sail and the prow of the boat cut through the waters of the Nile. Ramose breathed in the familiar air—moist, and laden with the smell of vegetation. He turned his face to the south. He was on his way to the very edge of Egypt and beyond. And he was eagerly looking forward to it.

A WORD FROM THE AUTHOR

PEOPLE who study ancient Egyptian history are called Egyptologists. They have written books about every aspect of life in ancient Egypt. Reading these books, I was able to find out what people in ancient Egypt wore, what they ate, how they travelled. Egyptologists learned a lot of this information from the writings that they found in ruins of temples, palaces and inside the pyramids. Some of the writing was carved into stone, some written in ink on papyrus or stone chips. Fortunately the ancient Egyptians liked to write everything down, so that a lot of writings have survived.

When people first started studying ancient Egyptians, they couldn't understand their writing. A single stone inscription was responsible for unlocking the mysteries of hieroglyphics. In 1799, a stone was discovered in a village called Rosetta. On it was a decree from the year 196 B.C. The decree was written in three ways: in hieroglyphics, in demotic (another form of Egyptian writing) and in Greek. Egyptologists were able to compare the Greek writing, which they could read, to the Egyptian writing.

It wasn't easy though. More than twenty years passed before someone managed to translate the hieroglyphs. A French man called Jean-François Champollion realised that the names of pharaohs were always written inside an oval shape called a cartouche. He found that this was true on all the temples and pyramid writings as well. Using this he was able to break the code of hieroglyphics.

After that, the writing on all the tombs, temples, papyri and stone chips that had been found could be translated. People began to understand the world of ancient Egypt a lot more. If the Rosetta stone hadn't been found, we would know very little about the way ancient Egyptians lived and it would have been a lot harder for me to picture Ramose's daily life.

GLOSSARY

cataract
A place where a river falls to a lower level in a waterfall or rapids.

cornflower
A tall herb plant with bright blue flowers.

crook and flail
The pharaoh carries these. They are symbols of kingship. The crook is a short metal rod with a hooked end. The flail is a metal rod with strands of leather hanging from the top.

cubit
The cubit was the main measurement of distance in ancient Egypt. It was the average length of a man's arm from his elbow to the tips of his fingers, that is 52.5 centimetres.

goblet
A bowl-shaped drinking cup with a long stem and a base.

gourd
The dried shell of a melon or similar vegetable, used as a bowl to eat or drink from.

Great Place
The area in Egypt which is now known as the Valley of the Kings.

griffin
A mythical monster which has the body of a lion and the head and wings of an eagle.

hieroglyphs
A system of writing used by the ancient Egyptians.

jasper
A dark green gemstone.

lapis lazuli
A dark blue semi-precious stone which the Egyptians considered to be more valuable than any other stone because it was the same colour as the heavens.

mirage
A false image of a sheet of water caused by light being distorted by very hot air in the desert or on a hot road.

nomads
A tribe of people who have no permanent home. They wander from place to place according to the seasons and food supplies.

oracle

A person who can tell what is going to happen in the future.

palm-width

The average width of the palm of an Egyptian man's hand, 7.5 centimetres.

papyrus

A plant with tall, triangular shaped stems that grows in marshy ground. Ancient Egyptians made a kind of paper from the dried stems of this plant.

Pharaoh

The title of the ancient kings of Egypt.

pylon

A gateway with towers on either side that get narrower towards the top. There is often a pylon gateway into an Egyptian temple.

pyramid

A massive structure built of stone with a square base and four sloping sides that meet at a point. The pyramids were built as royal tombs for the pharaohs and their families.

sceptre

A rod held by a king or queen as a symbol of royal power.

scorpion

A small animal with a pair of pincers (like a crab) and a long curly tail which has a sting in the end of it. The stings of some scorpions are fatal to humans.

senet
A board game played by ancient Egyptians. It involved two players each with seven pieces and was played on a rectangular board divided into thirty squares. Archaeologists have found many senet boards in tombs, but haven't been able to work out what the rules of the game were.

shrine
A box or a chest made to hold a sacred object.

sphinx
An Egyptian stone statue of a creature with the head of a person and the body of an animal. Usually they have the head of a pharaoh and the body of a seated lion.

tamarisk

A common plant of the ancient world—a small tree with thin feathery branches. The tamarisk plant still exists today.

underworld, afterlife

The ancient Egyptians believed that the earth was a flat disc. Beneath the earth was the underworld, a dangerous place. Egyptians believed that after they died they had to pass through the underworld before they could live forever in the afterlife.

vizier

A very important person. He was the pharaoh's chief minister. He made sure that Egypt was run exactly the way the pharaoh wanted it.

WHERE TO FROM HERE?

IF you want to find out more about ancient Egypt here are a few suggestions about how to get started.

The Internet: here are three great websites that will give you lots of information about the lives and customs of ancient Egyptians.

http://guardians.net/egypt/kids

http://interoz.com/egypt/kids

www.clpgh.org/cmnh/exhibits/egypt

The library: there are lots of books about all aspects of life in ancient Egypt. You can look up this subject under 932 in the library. Here are a few titles to start with.

Peter Clayton, *Family Life in Ancient Egypt*, Hodder

Geraldine Harris and Delia Pemberton, *The British Museum Illustrated Encyclopaedia of Ancient Egypt*, British Museum Press

Lesley Sims, *Usborne Time Tours—Visitors Guide to Ancient Egypt*, Usborne

SOME GODS OF ANCIENT EGYPT

Amun
The king of the Egyptian gods.

Hapi
The god of the Nile.

Horus
The god of the sky.

Maat
The goddess of justice.

Osiris
The god of the underworld.

Seth
The god of chaos and confusion also the god of the desert and foreign lands.

Thoth
The god of the moon also the god of writing.

The First Book in the Ramose Series

RAMOSE PRINCE IN EXILE

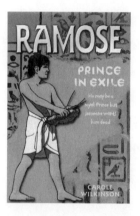

Spoilt and stuck-up, Prince Ramose takes his luxurious life for granted. He bullies his servants and is rude to his sister. But that all changes when to save his life he is whisked from the palace and forced to live in secret in the Valley of the Tombs. How will this pampered prince survive such a brutal place?

The Second Book in the Ramose Series

Ramose and the Tomb Robbers

Everyone thinks Ramose is dead and buried, but he is alive and trying to stay that way. He must expose those who tried to murder him and regain his position as Pharaoh's rightful heir.

But Ramose has been kidnapped by tomb robbers – who will force him to lead them to the hidden treasures of the royal tombs. He will be killed as soon as he is of no use. He'll need more than the luck of the gods to get out of this one.

Return to Ancient Egypt for more exciting
adventures as Ramose continues his quest to be
restored to his rightful place – heir to the throne
of Egypt.

The Fourth Book in the Ramose Series

RAMOSE: THE WRATH OF RA